Shaper

Shaper

BY

JESSIE HAAS

GREENWILLOW BOOKS
AN IMPRINT OF HARPERCOLLINSPUBLISHERS

The quotations on pages 81–82 are from the 1978 *American Horse Show Association Rulebook*, quoted in *Guide to Dressage* by Louise Mills Wilde (A.S. Barnes & Co., 1982). Copyright © 1982 by A.S. Barnes & Co., Inc.

The quotations on pages 87–89 are from *Don't Shoot the Dog!: The New Art of Teaching and Training*, rev. ed., by Karen Pryor (Bantam, 1999). Copyright © 1984, 1999 by Karen Pryor.

Other sources of information about clicker training concepts include:

Clicker Training for Obedience, by Morgan Spector (Sunshine Books, 1999).

Clicker Training for Your Horse, by Alexandra Kurland (Sunshine Books, 1998).

Communicating with Cues, by John Lyons (Belvoir Publications, 1998).

For more information on clicker training, go to www.clickertraining.com. For more information on John Lyons's horse training methods, go to www.perfecthorse.com.

The text of this book is set in Galliard.

Library of Congress Cataloging-in-Publication Data

Haas, Jessie.
Shaper / by Jessie Haas.
    p.   cm.
"Greenwillow Books."
Summary: While recovering from the loss of his dog Shep,
fourteen-year-old Chad tries to learn
how to control the family dog Queenie
with the help of a friendly new neighbor, an animal trainer.
ISBN 0-06-000170-4 (trade). ISBN 0-06-000171-2 (lib. bdg.)
[1. Dogs—Fiction. 2. Dogs—Training—Fiction. 3. Animals—Training—Fiction.
4. Animals—Treatment—Fiction.] 1. Title.
PZ7.H11133 Sh 2002   [Fic]—dc21   2001033368

1 2 3 4 5 6 7 8 9 10
First Edition

For Susan, Phyllis, Virginia, and Rebecca:
Greenwillow Past, Present, Future

1

HE DID NOT belong with them.

The vacation at the lake had proved this again, and every mile down the highway toward home reinforced it.

He couldn't go sit at a different picnic table, though. Sky would want to come with him. If he menaced Sky, Mom would shout, "Chad! For Pete's sake, be nice to him! You were four once, too, you know!"

Gib wouldn't say anything, just eat and grin, looking more like a teenager gone slightly stale than a husband and father. But Julia would say, loud enough to be heard across the interstate, "Four, fourteen—big difference!"

So best drift casually away, sandwich in hand, and pretend to study the rest area map. It stood apart under its own shingled roof, and Chad stood apart with it, stood apart in his clean white T-shirt—

He glanced down, his hand tightened, and mustard shot out of the ham sandwich. It made a chrome yellow splash down his chest.

"*No!*" He had only three shirts he could bring himself to wear, three blanks remaining from the failed family tie-dye business. He couldn't afford a mustard stain.

He took a step toward the bathroom and remembered the sandwich. If he took it in there, he'd never feel the same about it.

At the picnic table a shriek went up. Sky jerked his sandwich high in the air. It disintegrated in his little fat hand, and Queenie gulped at falling bread and ham. "Queenie, *no!*" Mom and Julia shouted, and Gib sat back, laughing.

The colors seemed to flare with the noise: Kool-Aid, Day-Glo, neon tie-dye. Every single member of his family wore some piece of liquidated Rainbow People inventory, and there was no way. Walk over there in his streaked white shirt and have Gib say, "Chad likes to dye things gradually"? Connect himself with them in the eyes of the old couple, the fat tourist family, the guy at the wheel of the yellow rental truck that had just pulled in off the highway?

No way. He wrapped his sandwich in its waxed paper bag and left it tucked in a corner of the map frame.

When he came back from the bathroom, he was yellow-stained and wet. Bleach, he was thinking, as he reached for the sandwich. Bleach might work. Two shirts were not enough—

A car door slammed. Chad's hand jerked back from the sandwich, as if he'd been caught stealing.

But that was stupid. He wrapped the bag around the bottom of the sandwich and took a bite, bending forward so any remaining mustard would splurt onto the ground.

The rental-truck driver came to study the map. Despite the heat, his khaki pants were crisp and pressed, and his knit shirt didn't stick to his back. Air-conditioned cab, Chad thought. But the man looked as if, no matter what, he'd always seem cooler than other people. He had a paper in his hand, and he glanced from it to the map, then reached out to trace a route from Exit 6, Chad's exit, off into the hills west of Barrett. Heading my way, Chad thought, but he offered no help. He wasn't good at directions, and he wasn't good at strangers.

The man turned from the map now, with a passing glance at Chad's sandwich. It must smell wonderful to him: home-raised, home-killed, home-cured ham—

Shouts gusted up from the picnic table: "Queen!"; "Queen-ie!"; "Hey, Gib, *get* her!"

Queenie trotted across the asphalt, toward the other picnic tables and the lane where the big trucks rolled in. Toward the interstate. Her golden ears didn't even twitch at all the voices shouting her name.

Out on the highway truck brakes whooshed. A big engine geared down to swoop into the rest area. Chad felt a jolt deep in his body, as if he'd started to move and then didn't, as if his insides had run into his outsides. The man beside him took a fast step in Queenie's direction.

But Gib crossed the tar in long strides. He nabbed Queenie just as she reached the truck lane. "Idiot!" Chad heard him say, before the incoming semi drowned his voice. He led her back, not reaching his arm down far enough. Queenie's neck was stretched high, and at every step Gib seemed to stretch it a little more. The man at the map made a sound under his breath, and his gaze crossed Chad's.

"People like that shouldn't be allowed to have a dog!"

Chad didn't answer.

The man went back to his rental truck. Get in, Chad thought. Drive away. But the man got a sandwich and a thermos bottle and sat at a picnic table, frowning across at Chad's family.

Mom and Gib packed up. Sky had Queenie's collar in both hands. "No, Queenie! No!" he shouted, while she sat panting tolerantly. On the way to the van, though, Sky let go.

Gib grabbed Queenie and hauled her into the vehicle. "Now stay there!"

Chad sauntered toward the van before anyone could yell for him. He'd just disappear behind it and never come out the other side. No one would notice. He slid past the computer box and pushed Queenie's tail out of his face. The tail was one more thing he had against her; Shep hadn't had a tail. He reached his seat by the back left window and looked out. His eyes met the eyes of the rental-truck man.

The man's eyes widened. His face lengthened in surprise. Then he nodded to Chad, just once. Chad looked away, feeling the heat in his face. Only when the van was in motion did he look out the window again.

The man crushed his sandwich wrapper into a ball and looked down at his hand. He'd gotten something on it, mustard or mayo.

He'd go wash, and then he'd drive down the interstate, take Exit 6, turn right at the bottom of the ramp, follow them up into the hills.

There were lots of hills and lots of people living in them. Chad didn't see many of them, fewer all the time.

2

AT HOME GIB set up the new computer. Mom stood over him, starting questions and biting them off. "What?" Gib kept saying. *"What?"*

"Snack! I want SNACK! IT'S SNACK TIME!" Sky yelled, in a voice that could melt the tar off the roof. Mom ignored him. It amazed Chad how long she could let a sound like that go on.

It was Julia who finally cracked. *"There! PB and J! Are you happy?"*

All of them were occupied. Chad slipped quietly out the door. On the deck Queenie wagged her tail. Chad made a fierce gesture at her. "You *stay!*" The moment he started down the stairs, he heard her follow.

He headed down the dirt road, hands jammed in his pockets. Queenie hunted chipmunks along the stone wall, sometimes ahead of him, sometimes behind.

Something was bothering him, something extra. What?

The rest area. The man. He felt strange about it, as if he'd done something wrong. But he hadn't done anything. Anything at all.

On the road below he heard a truck, Jeep's pickup. He knew that engine's sound. He deliberately didn't call Queenie.

She reared up on the stone wall like a golden wolf as the pickup came into sight, then scrambled down into the road. The truck kept coming, and Chad held himself still. He made himself look right at his grandfather, the square, hard face beneath the hatbrim, behind the wheel. See? See?

The big tires swerved just a little, just enough. Jeep raised his hand in that stiff way that was not even as lively as a salute and passed. Ginger, his Border collie, rested her chin on Jeep's shoulder and gazed out the back window at them. Her face, beneath the rifle in the gun rack, looked bored and superior.

Watch out, Ginger! Your time will come!

No more cars would pass. It was Saturday. No delivery trucks would drop off supplies or pick up orders from his parents' new energy-efficient lightbulb business. Jeep and Helen's was the only house beyond theirs, and they wouldn't have visitors, because tonight was the fire department's strawberry supper. The house near the bottom of the hill, the old white Cape, was still empty.

No, it wasn't. As Chad came around the corner, he saw yellow between the big maple trunks: rental truck yellow.

It was a lot worse than coincidence. It was fate that the man setting up two-by-fours to make a skid from the back door of the truck to the front door of the house was the man from the rest area.

Queenie's tail waved. In a moment she was under the two-by-fours, tangled in the man's legs. Chad didn't call her. One part of the earlier scene he was not going to repeat was the shouting. The man started and frowned at Queenie and then looked up.

"Oh! Hello. D'you mind—"

"I'll take her home," Chad said.

"No, I meant . . . would you mind very much just helping me in with my stove? It's the kind of thing you think you can do by yourself until you're actually faced with—oh."

He looked inside the house, following Queenie's disappearing tail. Chad could hear her claws clatter on bare wood. She's not really my dog, he wanted to say. I don't even like her. He heard her climbing stairs.

The man got into the back of the truck and hopped out a moment later with a leash in his hand. He whistled sharply: once, twice, three times. Chad heard a scrabble and thump inside the house. Then Queenie popped her head out the doorway, one ear up and one ear down.

The man fed her something and without haste clipped the leash to her collar. He lowered his closed fist toward the ground, and Queenie, intent now, followed it. He fed her again and handed the leash to Chad.

"Tie her to that bush, if you would."

"She'll yell."

"Yes, I expect she—oh!" The man smiled suddenly and shook his head. "I haven't introduced myself, and you haven't said yes. I'm David Burton, just bought this place. And you're . . ."

"Chad. Chad Holloway. I—we live up the road."

"And we met earlier today, didn't we? At the rest area. After what I said then, I don't deserve your help, but I'm glad for the chance to apologize."

Chad's ears felt hot. "It's okay." He dragged Queenie to the bush and tied her. As he walked away, she began to yelp, then to make that raving sound, like a pig being slaughtered.

David Burton didn't seem to mind. He'd maneuvered his stove to the top of the skids, and he and Chad slid it down into the front hall. Stairs rose in front of them. There were rooms to the left and right. Beyond the left-hand room was a second, and that was where they took the stove, skinning their knuckles on the doorways, sweating.

"Thank you!" David said. "Can I offer you—" He looked around the big, empty kitchen. "No refrigerator. No glasses. You're welcome to stick your head under the tap!"

"What about the refrigerator?"

David stood completely still, as if struck with a new thought. "What, as you so astutely remark, Mr.—Mr. . . . ?"

"Holloway."

"Mr. Holloway, what *about* the refrigerator? Are you by any chance offering?"

"Well, I don't see how you can do it by yourself!" The empty room pleased Chad, and he liked the way David Burton was coming to life. The effort of pushing the stove had brought color to his face. How old was he? Older than Gib, not as old as Jeep . . .

"I did imagine—that dog has solid brass windpipes!—I did once imagine that my daughter and I could move the refrigerator together. Having moved the stove, I now see—in short, please!"

They went back outside. Queenie achieved a new, poignant pitch. "Quiet!" Chad shouted. "Queenie!"

David Burton lifted one hand, somehow quieting Chad, though it had no effect on Queenie. "Save your breath," he said. They looked into the truck.

A forest of chair and table legs; dark, solid shapes of larger furniture; boxes, baskets, milk crates; beyond them all, the tall white shape of the refrigerator. David met Chad's eyes.

"Why, you're wondering, is the fridge in the *front* of the truck, when the stove was in the back? An excellent question! If you'd like to come back in two or three hours, I'll be in a position to benefit from your assistance."

Chad shrugged. "Let's just do it."

"*All* of it? That's too much! You'll have to let me pay you."

Chad liked the fairness, but Mom wouldn't go for that. You didn't take pay for helping a neighbor. He shook his head.

"Barter?"

"Like what?"

"I could help you train your dog."

Chad looked over at Queenie. Mistake. Her shrieks gained new strength and piercingness. "She's not really my dog. *My* dog—" His throat closed, husking his voice. Still, *still*, he couldn't talk about Shep.

"Would your life be easier—" David said. He was interrupted by rapid hoofbeats on the road. Chad stepped back, behind the open door of the truck.

"Chad? Chad! What's going on?" Gravel crunched under steel-shod hooves. Tiger whooshed his breath.

Julia. Julia in her orange sports bra top and tie-dyed leggings, her purple suede chaps with the flying fringes, her helmet with its black-and-pink polka-dotted cover. Tiger foamed at the bit, danced, whirled. "Hey, mister, that's *my* dog! Where's—"

Chad stepped out from the shelter of the door.

"What's going on? She's been yelping for twenty minutes. We thought you were cornered by a bear or something!"

"*You* sure would have scared it off!" Chad muttered. Julia didn't hear.

"So you're the new owner? I'm—whoa, Tiger!" Another whirl: Tiger's mane and Julia's purple fringes flew. "Sorry, he doesn't like trucks. I'm Julia Holloway, Chad's big sister. We live up the road."

"David Burton." David seemed colorless again. Everyone did next to Julia. He said, "If I untie this dog, do you suppose she'll follow you home?"

"If I gallop. But can't—"

"Thank you," David said. He crossed the lawn before Julia could finish, unclipped Queenie, and lifted his hand in a farewell wave. "Nice meeting you. Thanks for coming to the rescue."

Julia looked baffled. She wanted to stay, Chad knew, to pry. But David's hand was still up, waving good-bye, and already Queenie was starting to wander.

"Well, nice to meet you. Queenie, come on!" Tiger sprang away from the hated truck in a spray of sod, and Queenie lunged after him. The hoofbeats clattered away up the hill, and the yard became very quiet.

"The dog belongs to your sister?"

"No, she's—" *Why?* Why couldn't he *ever* get away from them? "She's the family dog," he said. "I don't want to train her."

"Are you sure? Because I don't have much else to trade. I'm

no gardener; there aren't going to be any bushels of zucchini coming up the hill."

Chad reached deep, for an answer that would end this talk and get them moving furniture, get them inside the empty, quiet house again. "The zucchini will be coming *down* the hill. That's what you can do for me: promise to take the zucchini!" He reached into the truck for a chair, and to his relief David did the same.

3

"This is too much for us," David said.

The refrigerator loomed at the top of the ramp like a vast beached whale. They'd walked it back, rocking from corner to corner to corner, then tipped it on its side. The truck springs still jounced, and the metal sides rang faintly. The slope to the door looked long and steep and terrifying. Chad felt too young to move a refrigerator after all, too small.

He shrugged. "We can do it."

"I don't think I ought to let you."

"It can't hurt us," Chad said. He wasn't sure that was true. "We'll stay outside the two-by-fours, so we can't get pinned."

David shook his head and stood frowning at the refrigerator. "If we had a rope to hold it back . . . but what would we—"

"Like a hand?"

The voice came from out in the late-afternoon sunshine.

Jeep, of course. Jeep in his green work pants and fire department T-shirt. Jeep's face was dark like carved wood, square
and clean-shaven. The bill of his cap was pulled low over
glasses that tinted brown in bright light. It was impossible to
know which of them he was really looking at.

Beside him stood Helen, small and neat in her skirt and
flowered blouse, looking young for a grandmother. She held a
loaf of bread. "Welcome, neighbor! We're the Houghtons."

"Oh, like the road! This is Houghton Hill Road, right?"

"That's right," Jeep said.

David hopped down from the truck. "David Burton." He
shook Jeep's hand—hard as a hoof, that hand, rough and
rasping as a file. "Did I hear you offer—"

Somehow talking to Jeep made David's voice jumpy and
cricketlike, and somehow that made Jeep smile, a narrow gleam
of white, even dentures, like a flash of sun on a cloudy day.

"That's what you heard. You take that side, and when we
holler 'ready,' Chad'll give 'er a shove."

That was artfully done. He didn't speak directly to Chad, so
there was no need to answer, or to not answer and rouse
David's curiosity. At the signal Chad leaned hard against the
refrigerator. It surged away from him down the skid with Jeep
and David bracing against the front end. A gulf of empty air
widened behind it.

Jeep and David upended the refrigerator through the door.
Chad heard its lumbering progress. He watched Helen peek
into the right-hand room and up the stairs, then follow the
men. Voices, laughter. Jeep laughing, bringing to mind those
gleaming, even teeth, those false teeth, and Mom telling of
the agony when, thirty-two years old, Jeep had every one of
his rotting natural teeth pulled in a single afternoon. It was

the only time she ever saw him drunk, and he stayed drunk for three days, trying to dull the pain.

That was a long time ago now. Jeep had the smile of a movie star, and something about David Burton warmed him to laugh, even.

Chad didn't stay to find out what. He let himself down from the back of the truck and walked home.

Later Chad lay on his bed, feeling the long muscles down his spine get rigid and achy from hard work. The television tried to outshout a radio program on the new computer. Sky played some wild game, thumping open the sliding glass door, racing down the deck that half surrounded the house, bursting in the front door. Mom shouted, "Don't run!" twice a minute. The deck was a full story off the ground, and running was forbidden, or at least she kept forbidding it.

Give *up*! Chad thought. He locked his fingers behind his head and pressed his thumbs over his ears. If only he had a door to shut out the sounds. Instead he had a blanket. All of them had blankets. Even the bathroom door was a blanket.

David Burton's house was full of doors: old doors with old iron latches, closet doors and hall doors, cupboard doors and shed doors. The kitchen alone had fourteen, counting cupboards and the two small iron doors in the hearth.

That house had been built long ago. Maybe no one had gotten around to building its doors for years either. Maybe that long-ago builder had stopped, once he'd got a roof over his family's heads, and thrown himself into making a living, just like Gib.

Chad didn't think so. That man would have been more like Jeep. He'd have finished his house.

Maybe David Burton traveled a lot. Maybe he'd need a house sitter. Chad saw himself spending long evenings down there, one bulb lit in a corner room as he studied, read, or just listened to the sounds of the hillside—

Splat! A suction dart whapped into the wall beside his head. Sky ducked back through the blanket, giggling. In again— *thumpf!* This time he hit the edge of Chad's mattress and ran through the room to the back corner. The walls between the upstairs bedrooms didn't quite meet the back wall of the house. Sky ducked through the gap into his own room and popped his head in again. "I got you! I got you!"

Chad bolted upright, grabbing at the clutter on his desk. Sky ducked back, giggling wildly from his own side of the wall. "I'll throw it!" Chad said.

Not that it would hurt much. He'd grabbed a plastic watercolor palette, six shallow bowls crusted with dry paint. He rubbed the dust off with his thumb. Brown, green, scarlet—

His stomach squeezed. Last fall he'd been obsessed with the sumac clump at the bottom of Jeep's field. He'd gone to try another version, to see if he could get something he was happy with, and he'd made Shep stay home so he wouldn't drink the paint water. He'd made Shep stay, and when he came back—

Queenie barked in the yard. "Shut up, idiot!" Chad said aloud.

Sky raced downstairs, and in a moment Chad heard the shriek as he was swooped up into the air and settled on Jeep's shoulders. Queenie kept barking. "Queenie!" Mom and Gib and Julia said. "Shh!"; "*Quiet!*"; "Shut up!"

"Good supper," Jeep said. "Should have come!"

"I didn't think the biscuits were all they should be!" Helen said. "Not the ones I had, anyway. But people seemed to like them."

She went on to the gossip, with an occasional rumble from Jeep. Fire department first: That was aimed at Gib. Helen thought he should join, and that Jeep, at seventy, was old enough to be done with volunteer firefighting. Never mind that Gib had tried and couldn't stand the mask on his face. It made him feel he was being smothered. Helen kept campaigning and comparing.

When that was done, she moved on to the new neighbor. Chad sat up then and stepped to his doorway.

Outside the three bedrooms ran a long balcony. Below were the dining room and living room, an open space the whole length of the house. His parents' bedroom, the kitchen, and the bathroom were tucked beneath the balcony, out of sight, but the view to the main room was perfect. Chad could see all of them hanging on Helen's words.

"He's divorced," she said. "Pretty recently. The furniture in that living room didn't amount to a household, so I'd guess he hasn't been on his own before."

She was a noticer, Helen! Even now Chad saw her noticing the dining room table that was an energy-efficient lightbulb factory, the living room that was mostly computer station, the walls. In a moment she might wonder aloud if it had been such a good idea to encourage the family to write and draw on the unfinished wallboard. Would paint really cover it?

Not likely. Even Sky, who couldn't write yet, had made his mark. Continuous lines, in different-colored crayons and markers, circled the entire house. Sky did them at high speed, not missing an inch, crossing forbidden furniture, charging through the bathroom no matter who was in there or why. At a higher level Julia's most recent tantrums and enthusiasms were recorded: horse drawings, telephone numbers, big I HATE YOUs and big I'M SORRYs.

As a background pattern, barely visible from this distance, Chad could find a record of his own ups and downs. Pencil scratchings, small and square and neat: "julia & pete wilson," with a wild orange Julia scribble over the top of it when she'd finally noticed. Four last-year's batting scores, labeled "Jeep, Gordie, Phil, Me." Lists of good books. Lots of bad drawings.

"The daughter's fifteen," Helen said. "One of these custody arrangements, I don't know exactly what." Gib shook his head, seen by no one but Chad, expressing mock amazement that there was anything about the Burtons that Helen didn't know already. "She was supposed to come tonight with the animals, but I didn't see any sign of it when we passed."

Chad felt his interest in David Burton diminish. Divorce. Furniture. A daughter Julia's age. David's arrival, after that encounter at the rest area, had seemed full of significance, but this was sadly dull.

"What does he do for work?" Mom asked.

Jeep said, "Trains dogs."

Chad drew back behind the blanket. That settled it. He wasn't going to get sucked into training Queenie. He didn't want her. He'd said so the day Jeep brought her home. Nothing, nothing at all, could make up for what they'd done to Shep.

Over the next week Chad didn't see David Burton or his daughter even once. A deer path overlooked the white house, and the walks Chad took to get away from his family, to make the long days shorter, brought him past fairly often. No one was ever outside.

From the overlook the house seemed small. The Polish woman from New York, that old lady with almost no vowels in her name, had done nothing to it, just moved in, aged, and died, while weeds took the lawn and the lawn took the drive-way and the trees grew close around. The slate roof, green with mosses, blended with its surroundings. The only change that week was that an electric fence went up in the sloping field behind the house and a horse arrived. Not only was the girl Julia's age, but she had a horse!

Once Chad walked by on the road. A cat sat on the

doorstep, an alert tiger that noted his passing with clear green eyes. Chad hurried on, trying to shake the feeling that right now, this moment, the cat was reporting him to Burton.

Thursday, as they ate supper on the deck, Helen phoned. Her tiny voice was distinct to everyone at the table. "Your father wants help with the hay tomorrow."

Mom's face turned pink. "Couldn't he have *asked*? We have a huge order to get out!"

"You know your father! The hay is cut: some for tomorrow and some for Saturday."

Mom said, "Tomorrow he'll have to make do with Chad and Julia!" She punched the reset button with her thumb. "It's like I never grew up!"

"We could become vegetarians," Gib said. "But as long as he gives us a side of beef every year and a horse for Julia, which he feeds, I guess he's got a right to call on us."

"He could *ask*!"

"Don't hold your breath!"

Once—last year, in fact—Chad had loved being out there on the high sloping field with Jeep. He'd loved the farmhouse and barn above and the way the dark woods framed the field. He'd loved seeing the far hills fade to paint box colors: Prussian blue, ultramarine.

Now the last two people he wanted to be with were Jeep and Julia, and the last thing he wanted to think of was a paint box. Down at the bottom of the field was the clump of sumac where he'd sat and heard the faraway shot and paid no attention. Looking at the sumac made his stomach hurt.

He stayed on the wagon and stacked bales. It was the easiest job and the lone job. He didn't have to say one word or even look down when Jeep or Julia might be looking up. He saw only the bales, maybe Jeep's brown hands or Julia's paler ones on the strings, then the place he was putting the bale, the green-brown scratchy wall he was building.

They stopped speaking to him. Soon they hardly spoke to each other. The only voice was Queenie's sharp bark as she and Ginger hunted along the stone wall.

It was late afternoon when the last bales were stacked in the barn. Jeep took off his BARRETT BASEBALL cap and wiped his forehead with his bandanna. "Drink?"

He and Julia walked out of the barn, the dogs beside them. Chad waited. He heard them begin to speak as they got farther across the yard. The kitchen door banged shut.

Chad left the barn then and headed down the road. In a few minutes he angled off through the woods, along the trail that ended at the waterfall.

It was small, only eight feet high, but the rock rim spread the water into a broad veil. Cool mist hung in the air.

Chad peeled off his clothes, braced himself, and ducked under the icy shower. He used his hands like scrapers to get off the sweat and chaff. Water splashed from his body into the pool behind him, and for a second Shep was there drinking. Not really. But the sound was the same.

His whole skin tingled when he stepped out, and the warm air felt welcome. He dried himself with his T-shirt, pulled on his jeans, and knelt to tie his sneakers.

The water caught his eye. Greens and darks slid like oil over the surface. Look deeper, and the color stayed still while the water rippled under it. Chad followed a dent in the surface till it vanished. Another dent, just the same, glided downstream.

Another. Suddenly the sound of the waterfall popped into focus, loud and constant.

Ow! He slapped his neck, and his hand came away bloody. Mosquito. Time to go.

He'd barely reached the road when he heard hoofbeats behind him. Julia had ridden to the farm; she must be riding home. He thought of fading into the brush until she passed, but he was bare-chested and already scratched from hay bales. He stepped into the ditch and kept walking, eyes down.

"Oh!" said a strange voice behind him. Girl.

Chad's heart thumped at the base of his throat. He hesitated to turn; would she see that? But he had to turn. It would be rude not to.

The big bay horse was from David Burton's. So this was the daughter.

She wore black, close-fitting black, and her body curved up like a sapling to a delicate collarbone and a long, slender throat. Her face was in shadow, framed by the black strap of a riding helmet.

"Hi." He sounded like a frog.

"You must be Chad!" Her voice was almost too low to hear. Chad stepped closer.

She was beautiful. Simply beautiful. Her face was rosy brown and smooth and soft, the kind of face that's hard to draw because the angles are so subtle. Her mouth spooned out a little shape in her cheek when she smiled, a dent like the moving dents on the surface of the pool. That shape would change when she spoke. He wanted to make her say something but couldn't think of anything to say himself except "Yes. I'm Chad."

"Thanks so much for helping Daddy!" the daughter said. "He's been keeping an eye out for you, but he hasn't seen you go by."

"The cat didn't tell him?" Oh, God, had he said that out loud? He felt himself go red, but the girl smiled, and he couldn't look away.

"Malkin? No, he didn't mention it!" She swung out of the saddle. The horse heaved a sigh and shook itself, with a flap and squeak of leather. "I'm Louise. This is Rockefeller—I don't know why. That's the name he came with."

Even on the ground she was taller than Chad. His eyes were on a level with the dip in her collarbone. He was horribly aware of his own bare upper body, so close. She must be wondering how someone this skinny could have moved all that furniture.

His shirt was balled up in his hand. Could he? He decided he could and stepped back a little and pulled it over his head, inside out, wet from drying off his body. It clung to him and smelled of sweat and hay, but he was covered. She started walking. She was going to walk down the hill with him.

"What kind of horse is Rockefeller?" Something to say.

"Just a mutt, I think. One of Daddy's experiments. He's actually a failed bucking bronco, can you believe it?"

"What?"

"Yes! Daddy bought him at an auction; he was probably headed for a dog food can. Well, several!" She made a gesture at Rockefeller's large side.

"What was the experiment?"

"To see if he could turn him into a safe riding horse. Mum—" She broke off. Sadness dented her cheek in a different way. "Mum had a field day with that." She assumed a voice that was harsh and angry, with a city accent. " 'Imagine! He bought a twelve-year-old girl a *bucking bronco*!' "

"Cool!" was all Chad could think to say.

"I thought it was cool! And Rocky's perfectly safe. He actually wasn't much good as a bucker. You know, 'been there, done that!' "

Indeed, Rockefeller didn't look as if he could muster the energy to buck anyone off. His ears flopped. His eye was mild and lazy and bored. But horses were deceptive. "Bet his name is really Rock a Fella," Chad said.

Louise looked questioningly at him.

"You know, *rock* a *fellow*?"

"*Oh!*" The look she gave him was surprised and respectful. "I'll bet you're right. I can't wait to tell—"

Rocky stopped walking and craned his neck to look back up the road. Hoofbeats. Chad bit his lip to keep from swearing. "This'll be my sister, Julia."

"Uh-oh!"

Uh-oh? Chad thought. *Uh-oh?*

"I'm not supposed to ride with her. Daddy thinks her horse might be a bad influence on Rocky. What should I say? I don't want to insult her."

Chad's mind moved too slowly to find an answer in time. Queenie came into sight, paused, barked sharply, and raced down the hill. Rockefeller waited calmly. Still out of sight, Julia yelled, "Queen! Come! Queenie, quiet!"

Tiger cantered into view, head down, boring on the bit. If he managed to yank the reins from Julia, he would bolt. He'd been doing that a lot lately.

But though Tiger foamed and worried at the bit, this time he couldn't budge Julia. She braced, biceps swelling, and skidded him to a stop, flung herself off in a flying dismount, and grabbed Queen by the collar. "Hi!"

Louise didn't look at her for a moment. She was watching how Rocky stood, head high, ears back tensely. When she turned, she blinked at Julia's black sports bra top and deep tan shoulders, purple chaps over tie-dyed shorts, polka-dotted helmet.

"I'm Louise. I've been looking forward to meeting you— What a beautiful horse!"

Julia flushed. "Thanks. He belongs to my grandfather really. I mean, he bought him for me to train."

"Oh, then you'll understand," Louise said, and explained Rockefeller's background, his need for extremely calm riding companions. Julia was fascinated. Chad walked beside the two of them, the two horses, Queenie, feeling as if he'd just become invisible.

A string of brilliant tie-dyed laundry showed through the trees. Don't look! Chad thought at Louise. Their house was hideous, a rough board chalet perched above the cellar/garage Mom and Gib had lived in while they built. There was a little horse barn out front and a brushy pasture and a vegetable garden. Parked near the road was one of Gib's old cars with a sapling growing through the bumper.

Louise's face brightened with interest, and she started to say something, but Julia kept talking, kept walking. Chad stopped, unnoticed, and watched them disappear down the road. Louise had taken her helmet off. Her hair was dark and very short and lay like feathers against her head.

She was Julia's age, not his. She was a girl. Still, this wasn't what he'd expected, not after that "uh-oh."

· · ·

The smell of frying onions filled the house. Mom stood at the stove, phone pressed between ear and shoulder as she stirred. "There's not much I can do about it, Ma. Believe me, we've tried. He's—implacable. Is that the word I want? He's like a rock."

Me, Chad thought.

"I know," Mom said. "I know. It's like he's shut himself down. He doesn't play baseball, he doesn't see his friends— no. No. He used to be such a neat kid. I know." Her dark braid, streaked with gray, moved against her blue and hot pink back. "Tell Dad we'll all come hay tomorrow. He won't have to go through that again!"

Chad went to the refrigerator for a glass of milk, deliberately pushing himself into her awareness. "Anyway," Mom said, "I'm in the middle of cooking dinner. See you!" She hung up. "Hey, dude!"

Chad just looked at her. He was meant to say "hey" back, but he didn't. Mom's tight smile faded. She looked pale. Not much time outdoors this summer. Even her freckles were pale, but a flush came up under them.

"Hey," she said gently. "You have to let go of it, Chad."

"Why?"

"Why? Because—because it wasn't anybody's *fault*! It just happened."

Chad couldn't believe how fast the anger took him, rising through his body like the red in a thermometer. "What do you mean, it wasn't anybody's fault? Did she *accidentally* take him along? Did Jeep *accidentally* shoot him? Didn't he know it was loaded?" He swung away, stepped in Queenie's water dish, and kicked it across the floor. It smacked into the wall on the other side of the house and water sloshed up the wall-board, turning Sky's lines into a drippy rainbow.

"Chad Holloway, stop it this instant!"

Already the anger was turning sick in Chad's stomach. It was too late to be angry, too late for any of this.

"The dog was in *agony*!" Mom said. "That's why—"

"That's why they have *vets*! Did you ever hear of vets? They're like doctors, only for animals, Mom! Why didn't he take him to a vet?"

"Because— Oh, *now* look what you've made me do!" She moved the smoking onions off the burner. "Listen to me, Chad. The dog couldn't be saved—"

"Yeah? We'll never know, Mom, will we?"

Mom closed her eyes. Chad watched her silently counting. When she finished, she turned back to the frying pan and scraped at the blackened onions with the spatula. "Believe it or not, Chad, I do know how you feel. He was a wonderful dog. But how long—"

She didn't finish, just dumped the onions into the compost and took fresh ones from the bag. Chad sat on the couch. His hands trembled, and his heart felt stabbed. He made his face like a stone, though, and Mom didn't say any more. A few months ago she'd have kept at him, maybe shaken him, but gradually she'd given that up. He sat there with tight fists, and in a while he heard Tiger's hooves on the drive.

A few minutes later Julia burst through the door. "Chad, he wants to see you! David Burton! He says if you can come down tonight, he has something he'd like to discuss."

5

THE EVENING WAS cool and violet-tinted. Silver songs of hermit thrushes fluted across the hillside. As Chad walked down the road, ribbons of cooler air brushed his bare arms. His white T-shirt glowed in the dusk when he looked down to slap at mosquitoes.

The tiger cat—had she called it Malkin?—waited on the step. It met his eyes knowingly and rose to its feet. Chad knocked on the door. Inside, footsteps. His heart sped a little.

"Oh, hello!" David sounded surprised. Julia got it wrong, Chad thought. He doesn't want to see me. But David was saying, "Come in, come in."

Chad stepped into the hallway. It was bare, not even a rug. Light glowed out of an upstairs room.

"You'll have something cold, won't you?" David asked.

"You should enjoy the results of all your sweating with that refrigerator!"

"That was Jeep."

"Jeep? He's your grandfather, right? Well, I don't deny I was glad to see him, but he only came along at the end." David led Chad toward the kitchen. No Louise there either; she must be upstairs where the light was.

A table and three chairs were the only furniture. The table was pushed up against the front window. It had a red cloth on it, a lamp with a glowing white glass shade, a green pottery bowl. The middle of the room was empty, and the kitchen seemed enormous.

David got three jelly glasses and a saucer from the cupboard. Malkin circled his legs, making remarks.

"Malkin's having milk. What would you like?"

"Um—" He could hear footsteps coming down the stairs. "Uh, milk is fine." She was coming. She was almost—

"Oh!" Louise said. "Hi!"

She wore a pale T-shirt and green leggings, and she was barefoot. Beautiful feet, long and arched . . .

"You've met, haven't you?" David asked.

"Yes." Louise smiled at Chad. Her hair was combed up into soft peaks, like meringue or like the hair on a Greek statue, a crown of standing-up curls. Among them a pair of small horns would barely be noticed. Chad took a long swallow of milk and tried not to feel helpless.

Louise went to the refrigerator. "Do we have any—oh, here it is!" She brought out a plastic-wrapped plate of something gray-colored and loaf-shaped that smelled like liverwurst. Malkin wove around Louise's legs, giving excited cries, then levitated straight onto the table beside the plate.

David and Louise exchanged a look. David raised his eyebrows. Malkin purred loudly in the silence, and Chad thought one of them would take him off the table. But they didn't move. Chad was aware of old house around him, of the dusk, of the fact that they were strangers.

"Oh, I know!" Louise said suddenly. "Chad's sitting in his chair!"

Chad half rose, feeling guilty, and David made a no-no motion with his hand. "You're right," he said. "That has always been his chair."

"But—" Chad's voice croaked. He cleared his throat. "Couldn't he sit in *that* chair?" The third chair was vacant, except for Louise's knee crooked over the back of it, her leg cased in green, like a long, strong stalk, her foot planted on the seat. Her toenails weren't painted. They were pink and glossy, and Chad wanted to stroke them as if they were little animals.

"We could teach him to choose any empty chair," David said, removing the plastic wrap from the plate. "Maybe we should. I hadn't realized that he considered that chair, and no other, to belong to him."

"If we're going to have a social life, Daddy, we'll need a fourth chair!"

David smiled a little sadly and cut a tiny diamond-shaped corner from the loaf. "Sit," he said, in a quiet voice.

To Chad's astonishment Malkin sat, purring so hard he squeaked.

"He sat!"

David gave Malkin the whatever it was. "Oh yes."

But he's a cat! Chad thought. He decided not to say it. It seemed rude.

David cut a larger slice of the substance, spread it on a cracker, and handed it to Chad. "We don't live like this usually," he said. "We had a little celebration."

"Pâté," Louise said, smiling at Chad. "Lots better than it looks!"

Chad took a cautious bite. For a moment the liver scent rose through his nostrils. Then a deep, spicy flavor, meaty and creamy and rich and light, made him forget that. "Wow!"

"It's expensive," Louise said, "but now you know. We buy it when something nice happens." She perched a substantial wedge of pâté on her own cracker and took a bite.

What happened that was nice? Chad wondered. And how soon would it be polite to have more?

"You went away the other day before I could thank you," David said. "You probably saved my life! Louise would have arrived to find me pinned under the stove—"

"And Mum would have done a victory dance!"

"Undoubtedly." David reached for another cracker. Chad watched him handle knife and cracker. Then he put the knife down, and Chad reached for it.

"So I still owe you," David said.

"Big time!" said Louise.

"But meanwhile, and the reason we're celebrating—" He looked across at Louise, and their eyes shone in the same way. For a second they did look alike. Louise's face glowed with warm color, and David's was pale; Louise's eyes were dark, David's blue. But their heads were the same shape, and they shared a kind of elegance.

"They bought Daddy's book!" Louise said.

David said, "And now all Daddy has to do is write it!"

Could you sell a book before it was written? Chad hadn't known that.

"It's called *Behave!*," David said, "and it's about the new science of training."

"Or the art," said Louise.

"The art of the science— Anyway, I'll need a research assistant, Mr. Holloway, and I wondered if you might consider the job."

A research assistant? The science, the art. The phrases jumbled in Chad's mind, and he felt a warning in the pit of his stomach, in the hollows of his elbows, and at the backs of his knees.

"What I need is someone to teach games to," David said. "Somebody to—"

"Manipulate!" Louise's voice sounded sharp-cornered and malicious, the way it had this afternoon when she was imitating her mother.

"A few hours a week," David said, ignoring her.

"But why not—" He couldn't say her name in front of her. He just looked.

"Louise knows too much," David said. "I need someone for whom it will be new, someone I can teach from scratch. Besides, Louise leaves at the end of August."

Louise *leaves?* That must be what Helen meant about the custody arrangement: that Louise would leave, that she wasn't staying. Chad remembered with what indifference he'd learned this. She wasn't Louise then, just "the daughter." He hadn't even seen her.

He noticed the hum of the refrigerator and the silence that surrounded it. David smiled across the table at Louise, a smile like Mom's earlier this evening, strained and false. Louise frowned back. Her eyebrows made velvet swirls, like crayon strokes.

"So I thought of you, Chad," David said after a moment. "You'd be paid, of course. Are you interested? I'd like to start soon."

That was what decided Chad. Louise was leaving. A moment ago the end of August had been an empty eon away. Now it bore down like a runaway eighteen-wheeler.

"All right," he said. "Yes, I'm interested."

"Great! The next step is to talk to your parents," David said. "Meanwhile, cut yourself a slab of pâté and a little piece for Malkin. Let's all celebrate!"

6

CHAD REACHED HIS room that night without a word to his parents; they were struggling to get Sky to bed.

When David called the next morning, Mom was surprised—and franker than Chad thought absolutely necessary. "I'd like to meet you first! We don't know a thing about you!" The words drove nails into Chad's stomach. David and his family, like bleach and ammonia, should never mix.

So, of course, Mom invited David and Louise to the farm for a picnic after haying. "That way we all can check him out," she said when Gib objected. "Besides, it's only neighborly."

"You think it's neighborly to unleash your sister on a divorced dog trainer?"

"I don't know why you always have to make comments about V!" Julia said.

Chad thought: this is going to be awful!

But that afternoon, riding the hay wagon, he felt fizzy. Louise lived on this hill. There, just below the tallest pine. Yesterday he hadn't known that.

It made even Julia tolerable. Uh-oh! he thought whenever he looked at her. Maybe Louise had walked down the hill with Julia, but first she'd said "uh-oh!"

Sky rode the tractor, between Jeep's arms and legs the way Chad used to ride. When Jeep stopped and got down to help pitch bales, Sky sat gripping the wheel, making loud brake noises.

Chad worked fast to keep up with the three of them, not building a wall of silence today, not doing anything but lift, heave, shove. His spirits sang, and his stomach churned. Louise lived on this hill. She was coming.

Gib talked: lightbulbs, business, fire department. The questions were long, Jeep's answers short, and Gib must be wondering what he always wondered: Would Jeep ever like him?

You don't want him to, Chad told his father silently. He reached for a bale Gib was struggling to put on the wagon. Gib seemed smaller than last year. Chad had grown, but Gib had shrunk, too, in his year of indoor, sit-down work.

Jeep didn't need help. Jeep was made of iron.

The wagon was about half full, the remaining bales scattered like dark animals grazing the stubble, when the long-legged silhouettes Chad had been watching for appeared at the top of the field. "Hello," David called. "Give you a hand?"

They weren't dressed for haying. Both wore shorts and sleeveless shirts and sandals. The sun gleamed on the downy hair of Louise's legs.

Jeep said, "More the merrier!"

In a moment Louise scrambled onto the wagon. She stood graceful as a heron, gazing down the field.

"What's that?"

Chad looked where she was pointing. A patch of orange-red stood out against the stone wall. "Fox!"

Everyone looked. The fox considered them for a moment and vanished. Jeep nodded after her, as he'd nod to a neighbor on the road. "Tractor stirs up bugs and mice, and then she comes."

"Snakes, too," Julia said. "You find them dead in the bales. Never grab without looking!"

"Yuck!" Louise shivered, and her sandals slipped. She clutched at Chad for a second and sat down abruptly. "It's *high* up here!"

Jeep looked to be sure they were sitting, then set the tractor gently in motion. The wagon swayed deeply. Louise's knuckles whitened on the edge of a bale.

"It's all right," Chad said. "It won't tip." She didn't answer, just reached for his wrist and gripped it tightly. Chad felt a sun blossom in his chest.

The wagon stopped on flatter ground. Louise let go, they both stood up, and the bales started coming. Louise reached for one and yanked. Her body arched upward, and the bale stayed where it was.

"Wow!" She opened her eyes wide at Chad. "No wonder you can sling refrigerators around! I can't budge this."

"Just roll 'em to me," Chad said.

"Oh! Just roll them!"

But she could do that, and now every time Chad turned there was the dark meringue of Louise's hair, her body bent over a bale, her beautiful curved wrists . . .

And there was everyone else, watching. Chad felt completely tongue-tied. Thank goodness there was work to do, and when Jeep pushed up the last bale, Gib, Julia, and David climbed on to ride. David and Louise sat side by side, arms wrapped around their knees, looking across the land. A long pink welt marked Louise's calf. Chad could hardly keep his eyes off it.

"It's like being in a painting!" she said.

Chad started. It was exactly like a painting, the one he'd tried last year. *Wagontop*, he'd titled it, and it was a mess. The dogs were the best things in it: black-and-white Ginger, auburn Shep.

Queenie, now; he'd use yellow ochre, raw umber, a touch of burnt sienna. . . .

He felt sick for a second, couldn't think why, and looked down the field at the clump of sumac, the sumac where he'd sat and painted and heard the shot and thought nothing of it.

When all the bales were stacked in the barn, they wandered outside in a group. Jeep swung Sky up onto his shoulders. "Look at the stock?" he asked David.

"Yes, I wondered who was going to eat that hay."

The barnyard was behind the barn. Shade darkened the lane leading to the pasture. The animals loafed toward the gate for their evening's graze. The red cow made a knobby silhouette. Her calf clung close to her hindquarters, but the steer turned to look at the visitors with dim curiosity. The old workhorse came straight to the gate and thrust his graying muzzle at Louise's face. She exchanged breaths with him and gently scratched his long nose.

"That's Billy," Jeep said. "Twenty-six years old. Lost his mate two years ago, and he's enjoyin' retirement."

"Is he past work?" David asked.

"He could work if I wanted to bother, but I don't have much for one horse to do, and since I don't work him, he isn't fit. It's work keeps us going," Jeep said.

They visited the pig, and then headed toward the house. V's delphinium blue Beetle was parked near the shed. Louise said, "I *love* these! Daddy, if your book hits the best-seller list—"

"Or I find a winning lottery ticket!"

"Whatever. This is what I want, except ask me which color, because I can't decide—oh!"

"Oh, what?" David said, and looked where she was looking, at the gold business logo on the door of the Beetle. Chad knew to the comma what it said: "Vivian Starchild, Animal Communicator. Lost Pets Found, Training Problems Solved, Psychically."

W_{HY}? W_{HY} W_{HY} why why why?

Why did she have to say, "Training Problems Solved"? Why did she have to park the Beetle logo side out?

Why did she even have to be here? V didn't live on the hill. She lived twenty miles away, and she didn't own any hay-eating animals, and there was always a spat when she and Mom got together, especially here at their childhood home . . . so why?

And why did Helen have to love those stupid tobacco flowers, which opened to beautiful white stars at night and in the daytime hung on the stalk like used tissues? One or two could be ignored, but Helen had to have dozens right next to the picnic table, looking as if they belonged in a wastebasket.

Didn't Mom own anything but tie-dye? She must have worn something before they started Rainbow People. Couldn't she dig it out? Did she have to laugh so loudly and have such a stubborn round chin and look so much like Julia? V, whatever else she might be, was beautiful, and she acted it.

Introductions. Too late Chad realized he should have made them. But everyone seemed up to the task of saying his or her own name. When David and V shook hands, Chad felt his face turn red. Even from behind, even from a distance, he could see David stiffen with reservations. Don't even think about her! he thought at David. *I'm* not psychic!

He caught himself sending this thought-shout and had to smile. He could still, just barely, smile. Sit tight, Chad. Don't do anything, don't say anything. David already wants to hire you, so just sit tight.

It was all he could do, though, not to rush over and intervene when V started talking with Louise. V regarded certain professionals with dislike: scientists, veterinarians, and most conventional animal trainers. They were arrogant and condescending to people like her. She must know what David did. Helen would have told her. Talk about the weather, V! Talk about the weather!

David wanted to know things. This was called Houghton Hill; had the farm always been in the family?

Jeep shook his head. "I bought this place in 1953."

"Did you grow up around here?"

"Jeep was an orphan," Helen said. "He grew up all over the place."

"All in Vermont, though," Mom said, as if anxious to correct a wrong impression.

Don't! Chad thought. He sat even stiller. Not those stories: Jeep the orphan; the families who took him in for the work an eight-year-old could do. Depression-era Vermont. Poor farmers. "Being poor doesn't have to make you mean," Helen would say, and start telling about *her* family, the saintly Minards. Hang tight, Chad.

"Whereas I grew up in Burlington," David said, "of which they say, 'It's so *close* to Vermont!' And my daughter is a Flatlander."

Now they talked about David and where he'd lived, and Chad could relax a little. There were potato chips on the table, lemonade, deviled eggs. One thing that would definitely impress David was Helen's deviled eggs— Oh no! V was telling Louise the rabbit story.

Chad had heard dozens of times the story of V's childhood epiphany. He mouthed the words as she spoke them: "When I went out to feed him, there was the hole he'd dug, just the way I'd seen it in my dream. He loved his hole."

Bun whisked in and out of his new hole a hundred times a day, showing many signs of rabbit pride. "About a week later I dreamed he'd filled the hole in. *This* time I mentioned my dream to Mom and Dad at breakfast. When I went out to feed Bun, I couldn't believe my eyes. He *had* filled his hole in and patted the ground smooth on top of it, and he was lying there looking terribly grumpy." This was the point in the story where V made her eyes round and still. "He never dug a hole again!"

"I don't know what it meant to him"—Chad finished for his aunt—"but for me it meant that dreams were true, that I should trust my insights." Louise's gaze was directed across the table. She had a small, secret smile on her mouth. Chad wanted to curl up like a caterpillar.

Now V would start telling about her life as an animal communicator, and Louise would think, as many people did,

Mom among them, that she was a complete fake. Chad didn't think that, but he didn't think this story showed the trustworthiness of dreams either. The story was true; it was also silly. It said, "Sometimes dreams can show you something. Don't build too much on it."

Ask! he thought at David. That was all he wanted: David to ask, Mom to say yes, and the two groups to separate, he going downhill with David and Louise, his family staying.

Louise, he suddenly realized, was playing peekaboo with Sky. She'd catch his eye, then move her head a little, disappearing behind the lemonade pitcher. Out again: peek. Sky's laughter squealed, and Louise put a finger to her lips. Sky's eyes got even brighter, and his laugh went whispery.

At least Louise wasn't listening to V, and nothing else awful was happening. Queenie whined. For lack of anything else to do Chad gave her half a hot dog roll.

"Oh, good!"

V's voice cut across the other conversations. She gazed at Chad intensely. When V looked at you that way, you felt seen, as if no one else had ever seen you before.

He wanted to slide under the table.

"You're getting over it! Queen is so happy. She knows it's not her fault, but she's been waiting—"

"*V!*" Mom said. Her face was red.

"Do you know how to skip?" Louise asked Sky, in the sudden silence around the table. "Come on, I'll teach you!" She and Sky headed across the yard, hand in hand.

V said, "Let it in, Chad. Let her love into your heart."

Chad felt hot and blinded, as if the sun had leaned down out of the sky at him. "Excuse me," he started to say, and he was pushing back from the table when V said, "Shep says it's all right. He *wants* you to love another dog. He fulfilled his mission on earth with you, and now—"

"V, cut it out!" That was Gib, sharp and angry. Chad couldn't move.

"He needs to know!" V said. "Shep doesn't *blame* anyone, Chad. It was his time. If he hadn't gone with Julia that day, it would have happened some other way. And he certainly doesn't blame your grand—"

Slap! Jeep's hand smacked hard on the table. Everyone looked at him, but he didn't say anything, just got up and walked toward the barn. Julia ran after him. She was crying.

"Well done, V!" Mom said. "It's too bad we all aren't as sensitive as you are!"

"My gift demands honesty—"

"*Honesty!* I'll give you honesty!"

Gib said to David, "Ironically, we invited you up here to see if you're fit to be our son's employer! I'm sorry—"

"No need!" David said. "What I want Chad to do—"

"You should know what this is all about," Gib said, overrunning David's voice. Chad couldn't move. His skin felt hot, and his insides cold. If anyone touched him, he would shatter.

". . . Chad's dog," Gib was saying. "Julia took him out with her on a ride, which she wasn't supposed to do, and he was hit by a car. My father-in-law came along a few minutes later and put the animal out of his misery. Chad—"

"I'll be *experimenting* on Chad," David said loudly. It stopped Gib from talking and Mom and V from bickering. Even Helen stared. "I'm working on certain teaching principles, and I need someone to teach them to, to see if they're . . . well, teachable. So I can't say too much more without giving the show away. It's games, nothing dangerous. But the cat and

horse have graduate degrees in my methods, and Louise . . ."
He seemed to run out of words for a moment. The hamburgers sizzled on the grill. Far off, Chad heard Sky's voice. He
could move, he found. He could turn his head and see them,
tall Louise and little Sky, skipping hand in hand.

"I'll pay him a dollar above minimum wage," David said
suddenly. He sounded slightly desperate. "That's what—
Anyway, what *is* minimum nowadays?"

Gib stirred. "It's a pretty good wage for fourteen years old!"

Helen said, "The burgers are ready. V, ring that dinner bell!"

Unlike in a book or a movie, the scene didn't fade to blank-
ness just because it had been embarrassing. They had to sit
down together. They had to get over it.

They had to eat the hamburgers that had been last year's
slow-witted steer, the one that had liked to lick Jeep's face.
Chad remembered Jeep out there on fall mornings, guarding
the steer so the horse and the old cow didn't steal its grain,
the steer reaching cautiously toward Jeep's chin with a long
tongue, the white gleam of Jeep's teeth, morning mist.

Then one morning, when the head had gone into the grain
pail, a bullet behind the ear, and now hamburgers on the grill,
hay in the barn, a new steer in the pasture, and a new young
calf at the cow's side.

Later, after David had arranged for Chad to start work on
Wednesday, and he and Louise had left, V caught Chad alone.
He wouldn't look at her, but the blue of her tunic glowed just
at the edge of his field of vision.

"Chad, I'm sorry. I think I was— No. I *know*. I was showing off."

Now he did look, and her eyes caught him

"You do feel better these days. Don't you?"

Chad didn't know how to answer. He didn't hurt every minute, so bad he wanted to roar with it. He'd felt gray for months; now even that was lifting.

But the world still seemed empty, and if the gray was all he had of Shep, then he missed even that, and shouldn't V know all this? Wasn't she supposed to be able to pick it up?

"You'll be all right, Chad," she said, looking deep into his eyes. "There's something very special about you."

Chad waited to hear what that was, but V had said all she was going to.

CHAPTER

WEDNESDAY MORNING, WHEN Louise opened the door, the door,
she didn't quite look at Chad. Embarrassed. He was embarrassed, too, because of the picnic and because someone had
let Queenie out and she'd tracked him down the road, catching up just at the Burtons' house.

"I'll call and have Julia come get her."

"Don't bother. I'll take her back." Louise wore crumpled
khaki pants and a dusty green T-shirt that said BALLET ROCKS.
Don't go, Chad thought. He could have killed Queenie.

"She's impossible to lead," he said.

Louise just smiled. "Daddy, where's the leash basket?"

David came from the kitchen, coffee mug in one hand and
notebook in the other. "Chad, do you remember?"

"Shed. I'll show you." He watched Louise's bare foot tread

on the doorstep. The stone would be warm with sunshine. A second later she'd feel chilly, dewy grass. . . .

Malkin rose from his perch on the stone wall, stretched, and came trotting across the yard. Queenie's head jerked up, and she bounded gleefully toward the cat.

"Queenie!" Chad shouted.

Malkin bristled, arched, and lunged. Chad heard solid little blows—*whapwhapwhap*—and *pops* as claws pierced skin. Queenie leaped back and ducked her head, swiping at her nose with her front paws. Chad saw a bright gleam of blood.

Malkin stalked toward Chad and Louise. His fur was starting to settle, but his eyes glared, and twice he whipped around to look at Queenie, who rolled on the lawn, sliding her head in the grass.

"Wow! Malkin, what a brave—"

"Don't," Louise said.

Don't what? Chad had bent to pat the cat, and he stayed that way, feeling foolish.

"Don't reassure him. If you tell him he's brave, he'll think there's something to be afraid of. I probably shouldn't have said that," Louise added.

Chad had a moment of deep disconnection. How much English did this cat understand? "Why not?" he asked cautiously.

"It's one of Daddy's things, and I'm sure he wants to teach you himself, so he can learn how to put it across." Louise picked Malkin up and scratched him hard under the chin. The cat squeezed his eyes shut and purred loudly. "Daddy's really embarrassing in grocery stores."

Chad felt logic slip again. He managed to put his eyebrows up, to look a question.

"Little kids are always falling down," Louise said, "and when the mom starts cooing, 'Are you all *right*?' he yells at her."

"*Yells?*"

"Well, interferes. He walked right up to this one woman and said, 'You're teaching that child to be a wimp. You know that, don't you?' She yelled at *him*, all right! I never go shopping with Daddy if I can help it!"

She pushed back the shed door. There was the basket of leashes where Chad had left it. He'd thought then that David must have a dog. It was weird—wasn't it?—for a dog trainer not to own even one dog.

Weird enough that he didn't want to ask. He looked around at the dark tangle of bikes and birdcages, dusty old furniture and lumber. A stack of doors leaned against one wall.

"Are these from your house?"

Louise shrugged. "All the doorways have doors on them."

"So these are spares. Did you know you have fourteen doors just in your kitchen?"

Louise's head came up sharply. She counted on her fingers. "I only get twelve."

"Did you count the little ones in the hearth?"

"No. How did you happen to notice there were fourteen doors?"

Chad shrugged. He didn't know, but if he'd known it would make her look at him that way, he'd have counted everything in the house!

She took three yellow plastic cubes from the basket, all in one hand. Her fingers around them looked like a study by Leonardo or Michelangelo. Chad had always thought the beauty in drawings came from the artist, but hands could look like that. The beauty was in the world.

In the kitchen Louise got a block of cheese from the refrigerator and cut about twenty half-inch cubes. She put them in a sandwich bag and called, "Daddy, I'm going!"

"What?" David's voice came from somewhere deeper in the house. "Chad, I'll be right there." His voice went on, lower. He must be on the phone.

Chad stood at the kitchen window. He watched Louise call Queenie, patting her thighs to encourage the dog. Queenie came, and Chad heard a metallic *click*. Queen's ears leaped from flat to upright. Louise gave her a cube of cheese. She took two steps. Queenie kept pace. Another *click*, more cheese. Three steps, *click*. Five steps, *click*. Queenie stared intently at Louise, as if trying to puzzle something out. They disappeared beyond the trees.

The voice in the other room murmured. Chad tried not to listen. The refrigerator hummed, Malkin washed in the square of sunshine on the floor, and time stretched. Five minutes, eight minutes . . .

David came into the kitchen frowning. Two patches of red burned on his cheekbones. "Hello, Chad. Where's Louise?"

"She took Queenie home. Somebody let her out, and she followed me."

David's frown deepened. "Oh. Well." He sat down and opened his notebook, turned a page forward, back. The paper trembled in his hand. "That call was from my ex-wife." He let out a noisy breath. "Do not imagine, do not imagine for a moment, that yours is the only messed-up family on the planet! That aunt of yours may be tactless and full of horsepucky, but at least she means well."

Chad felt himself relax inside. Everything was suddenly in the open.

David said, "Sorry, is it all right if I say your aunt is full of horsepucky?"

Chad worked out a sentence, and then he said, "That's one word for it!"

David gave him the same sudden, sharp look that Louise had. "It's a pleasure doing business with you, Mr. Holloway!"

9

"What's your favorite food?" David asked. They sat at the kitchen table. "Chocolate? Cheese? Chips? Name anything!"

"That pâté," Chad said. He felt funny saying the word; maybe he wasn't pronouncing it right. David smiled and wrote it down.

"Good choice! We still happen to have some. Now the game is this. I'll decide on an action I want you to perform, but I won't tell you what. You move around randomly. I'll click you for every step you take in the direction of what I want. When you get it, we stop for pâté."

"What do you mean, click?"

David picked up one of the little plastic boxes Louise had left on the table and squeezed it. *Click!*

"What is—oh." It was a cricket, a little noisemaker. You

pressed a metal strip in the box, and it made a click, the same click Louise had been making with Queenie.

"Every time this clicks it means pâté," David said. "I won't ask you to do anything embarrassing, dangerous, or painful. If you ask me questions, I won't answer. You're an animal, I'm your trainer, and I assume that you can neither speak English nor communicate with me telepathically. Okay?"

"Okay."

"Start by walking through the door."

"Now?"

David didn't answer. Must be now. Chad walked out of the room, turned around, came back in. He felt stiff all over. *Click!*

Chad stopped. What was that for? What had he done?

He took another step forward. No click. Backward. *Click!*

Another step backward? No click. Forward. *Click!*

"You just want me to stand here?" No answer. No click.

Chad turned in a circle. *Click!* Another circle. *Click!* Another; faster, slower. No change. All he could get was one click per circle, and he was starting to feel like an idiot. Also, he was getting dizzy.

He turned in the opposite direction. *Click!*

Okay. This time he turned one step at a time and paused between each step, listening. One click. Again. One click, at the same point on the circle.

Okay. He stood facing the back wall of the kitchen. No click. Moved his arms. No click. Stood on one leg. *Click!*

Standing on one leg? He tried that again. After a minute, just as he lost his balance, he got a click.

Again. Again he lost his balance, *click!* Again, *click!* Again—

"Aah! I don't *get* this!" He unbalanced forward, *click!* Took another step, *click!* Another, *click!* Step by click by step, he passed the door to the cellar and the bathroom door, and the back wall stopped him.

The clicks stopped coming.

Chad stood on one leg. Nothing.

Other leg. Nothing.

Turned around. Nothing.

Waved his arm. *Click!*

Wave. *Click!* Wave. *Click!*

Left arm only. Nothing.

Right arm only. *Click!*

Right arm straight up over his head. Nothing.

Bent at the elbow. *Click!*

Wave from bent elbow. His hand brushed the bathroom door. *Click!*

Wave. No click.

Wave. No click.

Wave. No click. Dammit! Chad thought. I don't like this! Wave. He brushed the door again. *Click!*

The door. The door. He touched it deliberately. *Click!* Ran his hand down it. *Click!* Touched the latch. *Click!* Opened it. *Click!* "Yes!" David said. "Excellent!"

"That was *hard*!" Chad slumped against the doorjamb. His arms and legs felt jangly.

"If you were an animal, you wouldn't even have gotten the explanation beforehand."

Chad closed his eyes, trying to imagine that. "How do they learn *anything*?"

"I know! And what if I had a choke chain on you instead of a clicker in my hand? This humbles me, every time." David got out the pâté and crackers. "Eat. It's part of your job."

When Chad had consumed two soothing crackersful, David said, "What we just did is called shaping. Take a small tendency in the right direction and shift it toward the goal, one step at a time. Do you understand?"

Chad felt loose and reckless, drunk on pâté and confusion. "I understand all the words!"

"The classic example is teaching a chicken to dance. I should say, scientists have a pretty loose definition of dancing! How would you do that?"

"I have no idea!"

"Chicken." David shoved the saltshaker to the center of the table. "It's moving around randomly, and I'm watching it, you should forgive the expression, like a hawk! It turns a little to the left"—he nudged the saltshaker—"and I reinforce it with a kernel of corn. Every time it moves left, even a little bit. Soon it's moving to the left a lot more often.

"Sometimes this chicken moves a little left"—nudge—"and sometimes it moves a lot left." David gave the shaker a hefty shove. It tipped over, spilling salt on the table. David set it upright again.

"I start giving corn only for the stronger movements. The chicken's got to take a quarter turn left to get anything from me. When it's doing that consistently, I wait for a half turn before I click, and so on. We say the chicken's dancing when it's making several fast turns. Do you see?"

Chad's eyes were on the spilled salt. Did he dare? This wasn't his house, but it made him uneasy. "Yes," he said, and when David turned away for a moment he pinched up a few grains of salt and tossed them over his left shoulder. It couldn't really keep away bad luck, but it couldn't hurt either.

"Now you shape me." David handed Chad the clicker.

"Um, okay. What's your reward? What does the click mean to you?"

David looked at him again, as if he'd asked an unexpectedly brilliant question. "It means yes," he said. "It means yes."

Yes? Yes? How did yes compare with pâté?

But David was leaving the room. What should Chad have him do?

Sit on the floor.

David walked into the kitchen. The clicker clicked; he was gripping it too tightly. David stopped walking.

Now what?

David turned around. No click. He took a cautious step in each direction of the compass. No click. He raised his arms, held them out to the sides. How *did* people start to sit on the floor? Julia folded herself like a campstool, but was David that flexible?

David bent one knee. Maybe. *Click!*

Bend, straighten, bend, straighten. *Click! Click! Click!*

Other knee. *Click!* Alternating knees. *Click!* Again and again. David had completely the wrong idea. Chad stopped clicking.

David squirmed and grimaced. He walked off the spot where he'd been standing, and Chad wanted to say no, but he'd been told not to speak. When David stopped walking, Chad clicked again, staring at David's knees.

They bent a little. *Click!*

A startled look crossed David's face. He bent his knees again. *Click!* Deeper, *click!* Deeper, *click!* He was as deep as he could squat. Now what?

One knee splayed toward the side. That might lead somewhere. *Click!*

David looked puzzled. He splayed the knee out again, again, again. Chad clicked. He could feel the grimace on his own face. His eyes bored into David. Do it *more!*

At last he spotted a tiny tilt in David's body, as if he were starting to tip over. *Click!*

David increased the tilt, *click*, more, *click*, more. He fell over on the floor and lay on his back. Chad could have screamed.

Anyway, he was on the floor, so *click*. David just lay there for a minute. Then he struggled up, trying to squat again. Chad had missed the fleeting second when David's rear was on the floor. Now he was squatting again, but tilting, tilting. Chad clicked him back onto the floor, and when David rolled up onto his rump, he clicked five times. "Yes!"

David heaved a huge sigh. "Oh! *Oh!* Boy, this is hard!" He lay back, splaying his arms wide, and gazed up at the ceiling. The man who'd seemed permanently cool at the rest area was flushed and rumpled, and there was a smudge on the knee of his khaki pants. After a moment he said, "What we just did is dolphin training."

It was English as a second language! Words Chad thought he knew meant something else in this house.

"You've seen those dolphin shows?" David asked. "Sea World, et cetera?" Chad nodded.

"This is how it's done. Think about it. You can't put a swimming dolphin on a leash. You can't yank it around. You can't get at it to punish it. Trainers worked out this system of conditioned reinforcers—"

"Um—"

"Sorry. The conditioned reinforcer is the click. We teach the animal that click means 'treat.' Then we pair the click with a behavior we want. Jump through hoop equals click equals treat. That's positive reinforcement."

"And that means—"

"Do the right thing, get something good. It's like a reward; only rewards come later. Reinforcement happens *now*, the instant the animal does the right thing. That's why we use the click. You can't stuff a fish in a dolphin's mouth while it's in midair, but you can say yes! and give the fish a few seconds later."

"Okay." That did make sense.

"The beauty of it is, the animal thinks it's training *you*. You get better and more prompt at producing clicks and treats—from the animal's point of view. It participates in its own training. You have a partner, not an adversary!"

"So, are you a dolphin trainer?"

"I'm a dog trainer, but I've used this on Malkin and Rocky, too, and I've seen it done with birds, fish, llamas. You can even use it on caged zoo animals. It's a new technology, and it's going to change the world. Imagine! Someday most trainers, most teachers are going to focus on what's going *right*! Yes! is what we're going to say most often. Not no."

He got up and reached for the clicker. "Let's do another round. This time you're the animal."

Chad left the kitchen, as before. In the bare middle room he paused a moment, listening. There was no sound of movement anywhere in the house.

He turned and made his entrance as an animal. He didn't see Louise again that day.

The next day they worked with Rocky. "He knows clicker work," David said, "but he's not great with strangers. Let's shake up his expectations."

So they went down to the pasture and clicked Rocky into approaching Chad voluntarily. It took time; Rocky was suspicious, as befitted a former bucking bronco, and had a wide range of cynical, disgusted expressions. But with enough clicks, enough carrot coins, he allowed Chad to halter him, examine his large yellow front teeth, and even swab his neck with alcohol.

"Alcohol comes before a shot," David said. "If we can get him expecting a click instead, he might relax enough not to notice the needle."

Chad had a feeling Rocky didn't miss much. Veterinarians probably smelled different from ordinary strangers. Still, it was interesting to click him into tolerance. He'd have enjoyed it more with Louise there to watch, but she didn't come down.

. . .

When he arrived the next morning, she was leaving the house. It was cool. Trees tossed their arms in the breeze. "Rain coming," Chad said. Thank goodness! It gave him something to say. "Should you get an umbrella?"

"We'll play inside," Louise said, and grinned at him. "Don't look so confused! I have a play date with your little brother!"

He has chicken pox. The thought came so clearly and quickly, Chad was afraid he'd said the words aloud.

"I always wanted a little brother," Louise said. "I don't know why."

"Me either!"

"Sky's a great little kid! It's a trade. You take Daddy off my hands for the morning, and I'll play with Sky!"

And I see you when? Chad wondered, watching her walk up the road. This was not what he'd meant to agree to when he'd taken the job.

That day David shaped him again. The moment it began, Chad knew he preferred being the shaper. First he was supposed to walk, and then that wasn't enough. He couldn't get another click no matter where he went.

Then he got one. "What'd I do? What'd I do?" He walked around the kitchen again, getting more and more annoyed, and suddenly another click.

"I don't *get* this!" Walk walk walk. *Click!*

Walk. No click.

"I'm doing it!" It was all right to talk, he decided. Blowing off steam was part of this animal's behavior. "*See!* I'm *walk-ing*!" He lifted his knees high in an exaggerated step. *Click!*

"That's it?" Knees high again. *Click!* But David wasn't

stopping him. He wasn't there yet. Knees higher. *Click!* Higher. *Click!* He added a little bounce to his step and got a click, and "That's it!" David made a scribble in his notebook.

"Agh!" Chad moved his arms in a sort of violent stretch. "This stuff gets you mad!"

David said, "In scientific jargon, you just experienced an extinction burst."

"A what?"

"Extinction burst. Walking stopped working, but it had worked before, so you threw a burst of energy into it. The way you'd do to a soda machine that didn't give you a soda. You'd press the button a whole lot harder."

"But why 'extinction'?"

"Behavior goes away if it's not reinforced. We call that extinction. If I'd stopped clicking at all, you'd have quit. Right?"

"That's been the game so far!" Chad's voice came out with an edge on it that embarrassed him.

David said, "In order to have something to shape, I need variety, different kinds of steps. I stopped clicking, waited for the burst—call it a tantrum!—and clicked you for that."

Chad let a smoldering breath out through his nostrils, hoping it was inaudible. "If you did that with a dog, you could get bitten."

David said, "If you were a dog, you'd have gotten a treat at every click, which helps. After your extinction burst you'd have gotten a jackpot, a huge, wonderful treat. So you'd be angry only momentarily, and then you'd be elated and trying to figure out what you'd just done. We've intellectualized it, postponed the treat, and you're still mad. Aren't you?"

Chad shrugged. It was true. It was in his bones. They wanted to move and hit and shove.

Red triangles flamed on David's cheeks. He looked down; his hands were nervously pushing the cap on and off his pen. "You need to know about this stuff," he said. "If somebody has what you want and all of a sudden the source dries up, that's a power play! When your normal efforts don't work anymore, you'll jump through hoops for whoever's withholding. Women—some women—are very good at this."

He'd had another call from Louise's mother. Must have; it was the only thing Chad had ever seen upset him. What was she like?

"It's all done by withholding," David said. "Withhold the click, and the dog tries harder. Withhold the attention, withhold the love . . . if it's done right, it just tightens the net!"

Chad didn't know what to say. Nothing like what David was talking about had ever happened to him. He was too small a minnow to be worth anyone's netting.

"When this happens to you," David said, "*when*, not if, ask yourself: Who's withholding what? Where's the hoop? When you know what's being done to you, you can decide. Do you want to play the game or just . . . walk away?"

Chad nodded. There was a space in the flow of David's words, and it seemed a good place to nod, a good place to get up and head toward the door. "So," he said, "Monday?"

"Is it Friday already?" David asked. "Wait a minute, let me write you a check."

The amount was larger than Chad had been expecting. He was completely vague about the money side of this.

"Thank you," David said, handing him the check. "Actually I won't need you Monday. This has been very helpful, but we need an animal in order to progress further, and the shelter wants to do a home visit and check my references before they let me have a dog."

"So . . . how long will that take?"

"It may be two or three weeks. I'd have to let the dog settle in for a few days before we started."

Two or three weeks! That was forever. Louise would be practically gone by the time they got started again.

With his hand on the doorknob he asked, "Does it have to be a special kind of dog?"

"No. The dog my former wife has now—my former dog, I guess you'd call him—is a terrier. So not a terrier. Otherwise, I'll just keep my eye open for a dog that appeals to me. The more ignorant, the better."

"Until you find one," Chad said, "what about Queenie?" His voice sounded thin to him, reluctant. He hated saying Queenie's name. But he'd hate not coming here even more.

"Your family's dog?" David put his head on one side, considering. "All right! Great! I'll see you Monday."

11

Two days of family. Two days of Sky trailing around, moaning, "I want Lou-eeeeze! Where's Lou-eeeeze?"

Chad had already forgotten the length of those empty mornings before his job. Attach an empty morning to an empty afternoon, and that was eternity. Two eternities.

In desperation he took his bike out, but there was noplace to go, noplace he wanted to go, anyway. Saturday afternoon he rode to the top of the hill outside town. The baseball game was going on, the pickup, adults and kids mixed together, all-ages, free-for-all game that he'd loved last year. Among the tiny, distant figures he could pick out Phil, and Gordie McIver. And Jeep.

He watched awhile. At this distance the ball was just a shimmer in the air. Was it caught, dropped, thrown to first base? He couldn't tell. Going down closer was out of the question, though, and not just because of Jeep. What would Phil and Gordie say? He used to know—close enough, anyway. Now, beyond being pretty sure they wouldn't ask him to play, he had no idea. Even wondering made him nervous.

He pedaled back home, and couldn't sit still, and couldn't read, and couldn't remember what he used to do last summer when he was happy. He took to the woodland trails again. At least there he didn't meet anyone.

Monday morning should have been better, but going down the road with Queenie, Chad missed Shep. Shep used to hunt along the stone walls, too, but it seemed that whenever Chad had glanced his way, Shep's warm brown eyes would meet his. It wasn't an Aunt V thing; he'd never wanted Shep to be more than a dog. But they'd said to each other with their eyes, "Isn't this great?" This walk. This day.

When he looked at Queenie, she didn't look back.

"Queenie," he said. She glanced toward his voice. Her eyes were depthless, shiny as buttons.

"David's going to be amazed," Chad said. "Bet he's never met a dog as dumb as you!"

David opened the door, and Queenie jumped up to lick his face. David turned his back, saying nothing, though her claws scrabbled across his ribs, and that had to hurt.

Queenie dropped to all fours. Immediately David turned. "Hello, Queenie!" His voice sounded gentle and pleased.

Queenie looked up with a surprised wag: Oh! Somebody's home after all! David scratched her behind the ear.

"And hello to you, Chad! Nice weekend?"

"Do you want me to hang on to her?" Queenie was sniffing the bottom stair. She was house-trained—she'd house-trained herself, really—but she looked as if she might turn up her leg and pee on something any minute. She marked things that way outdoors, like a male dog.

"There's nothing she can harm. Come on into the living room. Something I want to show you before we start."

Queenie climbed the stairs instead of following. From an upper room Chad heard Louise's surprised laughter. Was she in bed?

The living room held a television/VCR, a couch, and one chair. David picked up a video and bounced it in his hand.

"I'm what's called a crossover trainer," he said abruptly. "I used to train dogs the way you see little kids being trained in the grocery store—"

Chad's mind quoted Louise: I never go shopping with Daddy if I can help it!

"—jerk. The mothers jerk on the kids' arms; I jerked on the dogs' necks. 'Don't do this, or this, or this, or this!' A world of narrowing possibilities, till the dog hit on the one thing it could do to make me leave it alone."

He slid the video in and waved the remote. A title appeared on the screen. Before Chad could read it, David's thumb on fast-forward tore the letters apart.

A face next: David himself, younger. He held up his wrist with a choke collar around it and snapped the collar tight, speaking calmly to the camera.

"I'm telling you how one hard jerk is kinder than lots of little timid ones," David said, "how it doesn't, really, hurt. Pardon me if I don't turn the sound up!"

The face on the screen went on speaking. David said, "Now I explain that we call it a leash pop, not a jerk, and it's correction, not punishment."

David sounded sad and sour, but on the video he looked completely self-confident. He put the collar on a handsome boxer, demonstrating the proper position. Then he unexpectedly marched away. Caught unaware, the dog didn't follow. Jerk!

David took off again, again, again. Every time the dog seemed to be getting it, relaxing, David threw it a right-angle curve. Jerk! Jerk! Jerk! Jerk!

Soon the boxer trotted at his side, one ear cocked for the slightest hint of a coming change of direction. The camera switched to David's face.

"Here I exult at having gained the dog's attention." David stopped the film, took it out of the machine, and stood looking at the black cartridge. "When I made this, Louise was eleven years old, and I knew everything in the world about dog training."

Louise . . . how come it took her so long to get dressed? Julia took 120 seconds from bed to doorway. But that was one of the few beauties of tie-dye; you never worried what went with what.

"Two weeks after finishing this," David said, "I went to a seminar and came away certain that I didn't know anything, that I had to start all over again."

His thoughtful expression made Chad feel that he should say something, even if it sounded stupid. "Bummer?"

"Should have been. My life broke in half, right then. But I didn't know that. I was tremendously excited and relieved. I never had to do that to a dog again. I never had to say it was kind to jerk its head off." He laughed, still sour. "Like hitting your head on a wall—it feels so good when you stop! Let's work!"

He led the way back to the kitchen, got out a package of hot dogs, and began breaking them into a bowl. "What do you want to teach this dog? It doesn't really matter, so let's pick something that'll make her less annoying."

Chad shrugged. He felt as if there were an enormous gulf between them all of a sudden.

"How about sit? Does she sit?"

"Sometimes."

"Under what circumstances?"

"If you yell. If you push her butt down."

"This will be different," David said. "When she sits, she gets clicked. When she sits again, she gets clicked again. It's totally up to her how often she gets a piece of hot dog."

"But she's supposed to sit when we say, right?"

"That's the goal. Can we start there?"

Chad felt the deep itch of impatience along his bones. He was supposed to answer a certain way. He wanted not to. He always hated the feeling of being herded toward something.

But he was being paid, not forced, and any minute now Louise might come down. She should find him saying something interesting.

"I guess not. I guess we've got to move the ball down the field first."

David made a scribble in his notebook. "How do we move this ball?"

Chad bit down hard on his irritation. Baseball was his game, not soccer. The long, clean hit that drove in four runs was what he liked. In soccer . . . "You dribble."

"Precisely! To dribble in training, we take small steps. Where are we now? Where do we want to go? How many steps can we put between the two?"

"But why would you *put* something between you and your goal?"

David looked puzzled for a moment. Chad had to admit he found that gratifying. How many times did you get to puzzle an adult with a question?

"Ah! Word problem. What I mean is, we'll get to our goal using as many steps as possible. No strides, just baby steps. When I shaped you to prance, I asked in effect, 'Can you walk? Can you step a little higher? Higher?' Et cetera, till you were bouncing. That's called successive approximation. What we'll do with Queenie—since dogs don't sit partway—is wait for the whole enchilada and bit by bit gain control of *when* she sits until we have it on cue."

Scratch and slither on the stairs: Queenie was coming down. Chad heard a heavier sound that must be— Yes! Louise came through the door. Her hair stuck up like ruffled feathers. She wore a T-shirt and jeans and nothing on her feet.

David handed Chad a clicker. "Watch the dog. Morning, sweetie! Did you have a good night's sleep?"

"Yes." Louise stifled a yawn. "Morning, Chad."

"Hi." He wanted to watch her crossing to the refrigerator in her bare feet, making herself a bowl of cereal with milk, and a cup of tea. But his job was to watch Queenie as she grazed among the chair and table legs, snuffing up microscopic toast crumbs.

She neared the edge of the table. Hot dog smell must be cascading off it. Queenie lifted her head. Sniffsniffsniff. Her nose went above the edge of the tabletop. David said, "Push those hot dogs back, Louise? Please?"

Louise reached for the bowl. Queenie's nose rose higher, and her haunches sank toward the floor.

"Click," said David quietly. Chad clicked.

Queenie's head whipped around, and she stood up again. She looked from Chad to Louise, her dark gold eyebrows working.

"Give her a piece." David frowned. "Have you done clicker work with her before? She acts as if she knows—"

"It was me," Louise said indistinctly. She swallowed a mouthful of cereal. "When I took her home the other day."

"What did you do?"

"Just had her walk beside—by the way, she's s-i-t-ing."

Click! Chad reached for another thumbnail-size piece of hot dog.

"Toss it on the floor," David said.

Chad obeyed. "But she got up."

"Good. That gives her a chance to do it again and really learn what's working for her."

Queenie searched the floor avidly for a long couple of minutes. Then she came back to the table and focused on the bowl. A thread of saliva trailed from her jaws.

"Dribble and drool!" Chad said. David made a little laughing sound.

Queenie stood looking, stood, stood, sighed, as if settling in for the long haul, and sat.

Click!

Chad tossed a hot dog piece. "That was just an accident. When—"

Queenie went back to the table and sat, pointing her nose at the hot dog bowl.

Click!

"Three or four, Chad. From your palm. She's figured it out, and she gets a jackpot."

Chad bent with the hot dog pieces on his open palm. The touch of Queenie's tongue felt soft and moist. He wiped his hand on his jeans. "So, she's learned to—" Queenie turned to face the hot dog bowl and sat. "She's learned to sit facing a bowl of hot dogs!" he said. "What do we do, keep one on the table at all times?"

"Click her," David said. He reached for the bowl and set it in the sink. "Let's see what she's learned."

Queenie hadn't noticed the bowl being moved. She went back to the table. One look, and her nose lifted, rising and dipping to sample the air currents. Chad could almost see them, and a picture flashed through his mind, a painting he might do someday. A golden dog sniffing in a kitchen, the air full of purple and ruby and toast-colored streamers, rivers of scent flowing from many different foods . . .

Queenie sat, facing the sink.

Click!

"Two on the floor, Chad. Distract her." While Queenie's head was down, David put the hot dogs in the refrigerator.

Chad watched Queenie wander and sniff. He could almost see the hot dog scent spread out, thin and untraceable. Queenie looked discouraged.

Then she happened to glance at Chad. Her eyes brightened. She came to him and sat.

Click!

David handed Chad three hot dog bits out of the refrigerator. Chad tossed them onto the floor and watched Queenie snarf. He felt shaken. Queenie was stupid. Shep had been an extremely intelligent dog, and Queenie was—

She looked up, met his eye, and sat *at* him, abruptly, staring straight into his face with a cheeky, joking expression.

"*Jeez!*"

"Click." David said. Chad pressed the clicker, and David handed him the entire bowl. "Enormous jackpot. We quit for the day."

Numbly Chad set the bowl on the floor. Queenie's tags clinked against the rim. She pushed the bowl across the floor as she licked the bottom. It was a pottery bowl, cream-colored with a blue stripe.

"I love when they *get* it," Louise said. Chad started. He'd actually forgotten Louise was there. "That smart-aleck look!" she said.

"That's when it's fun," David said. Their voices came at Chad from out on the side of things. He seemed to be alone in a dark tunnel with Queenie. "When they realize they're controlling you—"

"But has she really *learned* it?" Too late Chad realized he was interrupting. "Shouldn't we make her practice?"

David shook his head. "Eventually, but not right now. Always quit when the dog's doing well and enjoying it, before it turns into work."

"Imagine if they taught math that way!" Louise said.

"Imagine if they taught ballet that way!" David said, and Louise groaned. She must be a dancer, Chad thought.

He waited uncertainly. How long had this taken? Five minutes? Ten? If Queenie was done, was it time for him to go home already?

Apparently. David seemed to have no further instructions. Chad asked Louise, "Are you coming to play with Sky?" They could walk up together.

Louise looked at David and shook her head. "You guys are through for the day, right?"

"Yes. Tomorrow we'll do more, but today I want to keep it simple for her."

Louise said, "Tell Sky I'll be up tomorrow."

It wasn't an accident. She didn't want to be with him. Walking up the road, Chad knew that. If he were in one place, Louise would be in the other.

TUESDAY MORNING CHAD met Louise on the road. She looked sleepy; the real Louise did not get up this early. It was hard work, never being in the same place he was.

She said "That was fun yesterday, didn't you think?"

Chad's mind jumped to the painting he would not do: the golden dog, the brilliant streams of scent. It would have to be oils, or acrylics, to get the intensity . . . and he was not a painter anymore, not any kind of an artist. "Yeah," he said.

"You guys are real New Englanders, aren't you? 'Yup. Nope.' "

You guys? Who guys? But Chad took the opening. "Nope!"

"Oh yeah? When's the last time you said a complete sentence to me?"

"Yesterday. By the way, Sky was sad you didn't come."

"Uh-oh!" Louise said. "I'd better get going!"

Brilliant! Chad thought, watching her hurry up the road. How to get rid of a girl quickly! If only he'd kept his mouth shut . . .

If he'd kept his mouth shut, that would have gotten rid of her, too. He went on down the hill, trying to think of things he could have said. Even now they wouldn't come.

That morning they got Queenie to sit in all the downstairs rooms. "They take awhile to understand that 'sit' means 'sit' everywhere," David said. "In the kitchen and the living room, *and* the yard, *and* the car, *and* with other dogs around."

"Nothing means 'sit' yet," Chad said. "We haven't said it once." All they did was watch Queenie. Sometimes Chad reminded her he had hot dogs. She'd sit, and he'd click.

"Dogs speak almost entirely with body language, so we should, too. It's only polite, especially when we're asking for something. When she's doing what we want, we can add words. Feels backward, doesn't it?"

"Yes," Chad said. He'd done it, he'd gotten "sit" out of Queenie, but part of him still didn't understand how you could *get* "sit" without *saying* "sit." And part of him did know. Part of him understood that words were sharp and weak and precise, that actions were blunt and strong . . . and just as precise if you only paid attention.

David said, "What does she learn when you say 'sit' and she doesn't? 'He makes this sound frequently. Maybe it doesn't mean a thing. Maybe it means stand here and wag my tail.' So we get the behavior first. Later, when we teach the word, there's a meaning for it to attach to."

Chad said, "When we say 'shut up' and she doesn't stop barking—"

"She probably thinks you're barking with her. What fun!"

"So if you give her a command, you have to make her obey, right? I mean, she has to shut up, or it's meaningless."

David said, "Imagine I'd moved in here speaking only Albanian, and I said to you, 'Gerzan. Gerzan! *Gerzan!*' and then cuffed you. You still don't know what the word means, so what have I taught you?"

It was kind of what David had done, moved in here speaking only Albanian. "What does it mean?"

"Nothing. I made it up. Let's move on to something new."

A few minutes later Chad was out in the yard, with Queenie's leash looped around his waist. Malkin, chipmunk, bird, interesting smell: She wound the leash twice around him before he could take a step.

"Turn with her," David said. "Get her on your left, and click that."

Chad unwound himself. To his left, Queenie was sniffing a rock. *Click!*

Her ears funneled at him. Chad tossed her a hot dog fragment. She gulped it and sat, eyes boring into his.

"Click that," David said. "Not what we wanted, but she remembers, and she feels pretty clever. We can build on that. Now move off, rather quickly. Sweep her along. . . . Yes! Click!"

By three steps, then seven, then more, Chad moved around the yard. Queenie moved at his side, eyes riveted on him.

"Now let's raise our standards," David said. "Try a turn. Click if she stays with you."

Just like the video. But where David had tricked the boxer into making mistakes, they tricked Queenie into succeeding. The clicks kept coming, and soon she was prancing at Chad's side, watching him joyfully.

"Good!" David said. "Try walking more quickly."

"Good! Try out on the road."

"Good! She hears the car coming but she's still giving you her attention. Click now and jackpot. Interruption of a good training session is punishment, so let's end it. . . . Morning, sir!"

"Morning." Jeep's elbow hung out the pickup window. His glasses had gone dark, concealing his eyes. Nonetheless Chad felt the flick of his glance. Jeep said, "Look, Ma! No hands!"

"We're teaching Queen to walk on a loose leash. It's looped around Chad's waist, so he can't accidentally signal her with it."

Jeep frowned. In his still face a frown was just extra stillness, a slightly longer silence. "Then what's the leash for?"

David said, "I like to think of a leash as a way of holding hands with the dog. When two people hold hands, neither one pulls the other around. It's just a nice friendly contact. A leash is also the law in some places and a good idea in traffic."

Jeep nodded, his face like stone. It was at the bottom of the hill, where this road met the main road, that it had happened. Jeep remembered. He must remember.

The truck engine idled quietly. Jeep turned his head toward Chad. "Ball game tonight," he said. "Want to come?"

Chad shook his head, keeping the motion very small, looking straight through Jeep. This wasn't fair, talking to him in front of David. It was cheating.

Jeep shrugged, looking out over his hand draped on the steering wheel. "Playing Westfield," he said, and waited.

Chad didn't say anything, and he saw Jeep move, letting out the clutch.

Chad dropped his hand to Queenie's head, to make sure she didn't step out in front of the truck. Jeep glanced out the side window and quickly away. Chad saw the hard line beside his mouth relax. Jeep was pleased.

Chad kept his hand on Queenie's head. If he moved it, Jeep would notice. His heart banged in his chest. The truck rolled softly on.

"Where does he *go*?" David asked. "With all he's got to do on the farm . . . but he's up and down this road a dozen times a day, sometimes."

Chad shrugged. Jeep didn't consider it work, raising a beef-critter, a pig, and a garden. He considered himself retired, able to drop everything to answer a fire call or run the road. He visited the general store for coffee, a farm here, a garage there, the friend with all the machine tools, the friend with the portable saw rig. He took Julia and Sky to their friends' houses, and he coached and played baseball. Other summers Chad had gone with him, alone or with Phil or Gordie. They listened to the stories, learned to use the tools, sat in the kitchens with the various cats and cooking smells. Everything had been different when Shep was alive.

"Sorry, none of my business," David said, and Chad realized he'd been standing there silently, that Queenie was pushing her head up into his palm. His heart felt hot and swollen and as heavy as a stone.

Later, walking up the road, he heard hoofbeats behind him. Julia.

He just could not take Julia right now.

He climbed over the stone wall and slipped into the green cave made by a low-branched hemlock. Queenie followed and lay down with a sigh. She looked tired. Not used to using her brain.

Out on the road the hooves made a scattered sound. Julia said, "Walk, damn you! *Walk!*"

Mincemincemincemince. The polka-dotted helmet jounced into view above the wall, and then Julia's face. It was red; her mouth was wide and square.

Crying? Chad leaned forward to look more closely, putting an arm around Queenie's chest to hold her there. Yes, tears ran down Julia's face. She jerked one rein, and Tiger's high head flew higher, his eye narrow and wincing.

"*I said walk!*" Julia's voice came out in a thin squeal. She put both reins into one hand for a moment to wipe at her face. Tiger ducked his head, snatching rein, trotting more strongly. "I *hate* you!" Julia said breathlessly. Chad could only see her back now. "I wish I could sell you!" *Mincemince-mincemince*, they jigged on up the road.

Chad sat back against the hemlock trunk. Light came through the branches, making shifting spangles on the ground around him. He didn't know what to think about what he'd just seen. What did Julia want, and why? She was a brilliant rider. He'd seen Tiger make good-faith efforts to unload her, and she'd never shown daylight between butt and saddle. She didn't *need* the horse to walk. She could stick to him through anything.

Queenie's ears pricked toward the road. Chad heard the soft crunch of footsteps, hardly a sound at all. It must be Louise, but not even the peaks of her hair showed above the stone wall.

He could catch up with her—

And say what? He'd felt at first that he was interesting to her, but that seemed to have worn off. He was too old to be a little brother and evidently too young to be anything else.

WEDNESDAY DAVID BEGAN introducing the word *sit*, having Chad say it just as Queenie tucked her haunches. Within eight repetitions she sat at the word. She had a new, warm glow in her eyes.

"This is when the universe becomes coherent for them," David said. "I call it the Why Didn't You Say So Before? stage."

Indeed, Queenie's quickness was almost a rebuke. It was the kind of quickness Chad saw in smart girls at school, who answered questions before the teacher finished asking. If you wanted to train Queenie, you'd have to work hard to keep ahead of her. A strange thought: scrambling to keep mentally ahead of Queenie! Good thing he didn't want to train her. His job was to learn what David told him. Queenie was just a prop.

At noontime she bounded to greet Louise, ears flattened,

her whole body a golden arc of joy. If he were a dog, Chad could do that, too. No one would expect him to hide his feelings. If he were a dog, Louise would like him. He'd love her, and she'd like him for that, and everything would be simple.

"Hi," he said, and passed her, and was astonished at how much that hurt.

That night at supper he noticed new writing on the wall beside the table: neatly penciled "Sky" and "Louise." Below, Sky level, a sprawling row of purple crayon *L*'s looped around the corner.

"Who do you want at your birthday party?" Mom asked Julia, as she dished out the ice cream. "Time to think about inviting people."

"Pia and Chess will still be at camp," Julia said, and Mom and Gib looked at each other. Horse camp had been the big issue this spring. Julia had assumed she was going. She'd even filled out her application, only to discover that there wasn't enough money.

"I'll ask Louise," Julia said.

"LOUISE!" Sky shouted, and Mom said, "Or we could wait till Pia and Chess are back—"

"No, just Louise."

"We can play AMBUSH! BANG BANG—"

Mom said, "On Julia's birthday we should do things *she* wants to do."

"Julia likes to play with me when Louise is here."

Gib smiled and tried to hide it, and Julia said, "When Louise is here, you play quietly!"

"I don't know how she does that," Mom said.

"You *have* to whisper!" Sky said. His eyes were round as blueberries. "So the bad guys don't know you're there!"

"Of course," Mom said. "I don't know why I never thought of that! Julia, what do you want—"

"I hide better than anybody," Sky said. "Louise says the best ambushers know how to wait a long, long time. Sometimes they get itches and they don't even scratch them, and they might have to cough, but they even cough quiet. See how quiet I can cough?"

"Not even an ant could cough quieter," Gib said. "The girl's a genius."

She sure was! Chad could see, as if someone had drawn him a diagram, how Louise had trained Sky. Trained him and made him like it.

"So what do you want for your birthday?" Mom asked.

Julia flushed and frowned. "A gift certificate from the tack shop. Then I can pick."

She wanted something she didn't dare ask for. Chad knew the signs. Probably something expensive. What she needed was training lessons. Chad was getting those, and Julia got to be with Louise, and it looked as if someone Up There had a sick sense of humor. Chad pushed back from the table.

"Hey, Chad, what you up to?" Gib tilted his head to one side. His ponytail with its multiple bindings of elastic looped over his shoulder: picture of an open and accessible New Age dad.

Chad shrugged and went upstairs. As he passed above them on the landing, he heard his parents' hushed voices, talking about him again.

"He just wants to be the center of attention!" Julia said loudly.

All right! Chad thought. All right.

When Julia went downstairs that evening, and the shower

started, he slipped through the gap in their wall, into her room.

For a long time now he'd only wanted Julia to go away. He didn't want to bug her, or spy on her, or be anywhere near her. For more than six months he hadn't been in here.

It was a mess, of course. A bright, clashing heap of clothes covered half the floor, like an anthill. Books were stacked by the bed and in tall, slithery piles on the desk, and everywhere on the wall were horses.

But something gave the room a hushed, dark feeling. It made Chad uneasy. He ducked back through the wall and stood listening. Yes, the shower still ran. He stepped through the gap again, eyes and ears wide.

Dark. Cool. The chaos that was Julia was all over the floor, but on the walls . . .

It was the posters. Riders in spotless white and gleaming black. Big, powerful horses, with the veins popped out on their necks and shoulders. What were they doing? They all looked compressed, not by outside force but by something within themselves, a great calm gathering of power that was like— What was it like?

Like a tom turkey strutting. Like Jeep's old horse when Tiger arrived and he swelled himself up and pranced around with his skimpy black tail streaming. Like Jeep himself walking into the fire station or onto the ballfield.

There were quotes written on the wallboard beneath the posters: "Calm, forward, and straight"; "Anyone who loves his horse will be patient"; "No serious struggle should ever arise during the training of young horses."

Beneath a photo of Tiger was a long one that read: "Dressage . . . the gradual harmonious development of the horse's physical and mental condition with the aim to achieve . . . a perfect understanding with its rider. . . . the horse obeys willingly and without hesitation. . . . The horse . . . does not need the visible aids of the rider. (. . . from the 1978 *AHSA Rulebook*)."

Julia was as far from that as she could possibly be.

A movement in the mirror caught Chad's eyes. Himself, looking both lanky and knotted at the joints, as if much of him lay coiled there, waiting to expand. He was smiling. He hadn't realized that. The corners of his mouth looked sharp and nervous and full of unpleasant relish. The smile vanished when he looked at it, not caring to be seen.

He turned away from himself and spotted a catalog by the bed: plastic horse models. Julia used to get one for her birthday every year. They were amazingly lifelike. Back when he'd considered himself an artist, Chad had borrowed them occasionally to draw from. Unlike a real horse, they would stand still.

He crouched to look. One was circled in green marker, a chestnut Morgan that looked like Tiger. This was it! This was what Julia wanted and didn't dare ask for. Not too expensive, too babyish—

The stairs creaked. He'd forgotten to listen! He took two long soft-footed steps across the room, and on the third came down on something sharp. He kept going, ducked through the gap, and was standing by his own desk when Julia's bare feet went by. She flicked at his blanket, showing him she could look in any time she wanted, but the feet didn't slow. She went on into her room and noticed nothing.

C H A P T E R

14

T HURSDAY DAVID LET Queenie wander around his house. Whenever she accidentally came to Chad, she was clicked and treated. "It's a start on getting her to come when called," David said. "This isn't the normal sequence I'd use, but we're trying to kill three birds with one stone: teach you the concepts, teach me how to teach the concepts, and teach Queenie a few things that'll make your life easier."

Chad felt a darkening within him, as swift, sudden, and precise as a cloud sailing across the face of the sun. "Would your life be easier—" David had begun to ask that first day at the rear of the crowded moving van. Chad had said no, and he'd been right. Nothing about training Queenie was making his life easier!

He left early, before David was ready to have him go. If he

got home while Louise was still there, maybe he could be part of things. He'd even play ambush, if that was what it took.

From the driveway he heard the sound of voices. One was Julia's, almost unrecognizable at this pitch. They were on the deck. Now where was Queenie? She could run ahead, announce him; that would be useful. But a chipmunk had insulted her from the stone wall, and she was trying to dig it out. Chad went into the yard where he could see them. They'd see him, too. Maybe Louise would look glad.

Neither noticed. Their heads bent over a magazine. When Louise looked up, it was to speak to Julia, with a smile. They were friends. He'd seen Louise first, but Sky and Julia had her.

Chad ducked under the deck and threaded between bicycles, garbage cans, and sections of woodpile till he was beneath them and could hear perfectly. It was simple justice that they weren't talking about anything interesting. Was this one cool? Was this one cooler? Boys or bathing suits—Chad couldn't tell.

Out of the blue Julia asked, "So what is it like, having a trainer for a father?"

"I don't know."

"What do you mean, you don't know? You have to know!"

Louise said, "No. I'm just me. I'm not me *and* you, or me *and* somebody else. So how can I compare?"

"Well, all right," Julia said. "But what is it *like?* Do you think he treats you like a dog?" Some people would have laughed, saying that, but a sense of humor wasn't built into Julia.

Louise said, "It's . . . nice. Daddy makes it easy for me to do what he wants. He makes sure that works for me, gets me what *I* want. So we're both happy."

"Oh."

"It's not what you're thinking!" Louise said. "Daddy gets me to do things, and it doesn't feel like 'making' me. It feels like what I wanted to do, anyway."

"Is it a one-way street?" Julia sounded angry. "Or do you do it back?"

"Oh yes! We're both very manipulative!"

"I'd say so!"

"There's Queenie," Louise said, in a withdrawing voice. "Chad must be here. I'd better get back."

Their feet moved above him. Chad stepped closer to the foundation. He felt cold down his center, cold and slowed down like a frog on a frosty morning. *We're both very manipulative.*

Yes. That they were. From the moment he'd met them they'd gotten him to do things, things he'd thought he wanted to do, anyway. It hadn't made him happy, though. All the others got what they wanted, and he walked down the hill every morning to train a dog he didn't like.

As David had always intended.

The next morning the lawn with its patches of purple weed, the green dent of a driveway, the low house looking as if it had grown out of the lawn, didn't seem magical anymore. Not good magic, anyway. More like the kind of place a lonely traveler might come upon unawares, knock on the door, as Chad knocked now, and be let in, as David let him in, and never come out from again.

He followed David to the kitchen with his eyes wide open. In the bare middle room he squinted at the titles of the books, lined up in rows on the floor. *On Behavior. Clicker Magic! Beyond Obedience. Don't Shoot—*

What? His shocked eyes flinched away for a second.

Don't Shoot the Dog! That was actually the title of a book—no, two, a big paperback and a little one. Queenie's tags jingled behind him. A chill settled between his shoulder blades. The book must have been there all along, but this was the first time he'd seen it. He'd been stupid. There'd be a price.

Louise sat at the table, in a deeply plush terry-cloth bathrobe. Her face was sleepy-looking, her hair rumpled. Chad looked out the window, at the yard closed around by trees, and wished he could go away.

But it was Louise who went. She gathered up her breakfast dishes and put them in the sink, and she went off upstairs. Hyperalert, Chad listened to her footsteps while David set up a lesson for him and Queenie. Louise came back downstairs, paused in the hallway, and then the door opened and shut. He and Queenie were alone with David.

Who was saying, "You might want to consider changing her name."

Chad pushed some words out, hardly caring what they were. "Isn't that bad luck?"

"Her name is a cue, not her identity. And it's a cue you guys have pretty much burned."

He was supposed to be curious but clueless now. He was supposed to say, "What do you mean?" So he did, thinking that David had to hear the dullness in his voice.

But David said, "Burning a cue? It's like keeping your finger on the on switch till you fry the electronics. By using it without actually getting her attention, you've turned her name into background noise. So a new name would help. But if you don't like the idea, we can work on resensitizing— Is this a bad time for you?"

"Huh?"

"You seem distracted. Would you rather not—"

"No," Chad said. "Let's get started."

"Does this work on people?" he asked later. It seemed like good timing. David was bent over his notebook, scribbling. He might answer without paying too much attention.

But David looked full into Chad's face. His eyes were bright and unreadable. "You mean, beyond what we did the first few days? Definitely yes! It can be used to your harm, and it can be used for your good." He went into the next room and came back with the big paperback, *Don't Shoot the Dog!* It bristled with bookmarks. David scanned the pages. "Here, and"—he checked in the index—"here."

Chad took the book gingerly, his fingers avoiding the title words. David had marked the story of a young woman who tamed her bossy husband and father-in-law: "The daughter formed a practice of responding minimally to commands and harsh remarks, while reinforcing with approval and affection any tendency by either man to be pleasant or thoughtful. In a year she had turned them into decent human beings. Now they greet her with smiles when she comes home and leap up—both of them—to help with the groceries."

Isn't that nice! Decent human beings!

David was writing in his notebook again. Where did this author talk about shooting dogs? Chad flipped through quickly but found nothing. David looked about to finish; he opened to the page he was supposed to read.

Some sentences were underlined. ". . . it is easier to notice mistakes than to notice improvement.

". . . if you are calculating to shape someone's behavior, it is very tempting to talk about it. And talking about it can ruin it . . . you better not brag about it later, either."

Chad looked up from the book. Queenie lay staring at him. Her eyes glowed; they connected with him. A week ago that never happened, and Chad would have believed it never could.

For a moment he felt the way he had when he snuck Jeep's beer once. The world seemed to float, or else he was floating, no thoughts in his head, just an unformed wondering, like a lazy question mark made of smoke.

He looked reluctantly back at the underlined sentences: ". . . isn't it possible to shape people to do horrible things? Yes, indeed. . . . Let the photographs of Patty Hearst, holding a machine gun in a bank robbery, be evidence. But while her captors did not need a book to tell them how to do that, would we not all be better defended against such events if we understood, each of us, how the laws of shaping work?"

Chad found that he was nodding, slow and wide-eyed. Yes, that was what he needed to be: better defended.

"Would you like to borrow that?" David asked. "I have several copies. It's my bible." He paused and sighed. "It's so good that truthfully I wonder if I have anything to add."

Chad knew the right thing to say: "Your publisher must think so." He took a breath to, but then he didn't. The deflated look settled on David's face. Chad felt that sharp-cornered smile on his mouth and with one hand smoothed it away.

David said, "I tell myself there's value in stating things a different way. Everybody learns differently. Maybe my words will click for someone who doesn't get this. Don't you think?"

Chad just shrugged.

David looked even more dispirited. "Guess it's time to

write your paycheck." No invitation to have a bite of lunch, as on other days. Chad had done that. By not responding, he'd shaped David, backed him off, muted him.

His laughter came as a silent snort, rocking him. A moment ago he'd been small and confused and in danger. Now he was the danger. He was in control. David might know shaping inside out, but even he was helpless to evade it, and he'd made a mistake. Showing Chad that book, he'd bragged. Without meaning to, he'd given the show away.

Now he bent over the table, writing out Chad's check. Chad gazed at his back. What next? This power should be used. He should get . . .

The front door banged. Chad took half a step back from David as Louise came into the room, warm and glowing. He felt as if he'd been caught at something.

"Daddy! Hi, Chad. Daddy, I just figured out what you can give Chad! For helping you with the stove!"

"You don't—" Chad's interruption wasn't loud enough. He might have power over David, but he was helpless with Louise; she wasn't listening.

"A door! They don't have any doors in his house, not even on the bedrooms. Have a door, Chad! Be the first on your block!"

He'd already reached for the check, and he felt it, thin between his thumb and forefinger, as he stared at her. Laughing at him. Laughing at his family. Here in their kitchen with its fourteen doors.

He dropped the check. It fluttered toward the floor.

"You can keep your damned doors!" he said, and walked out, snapping his fingers for Queenie.

15

IT HAPPENED SO quickly that all the rest of that day he needed to relive it.

"You can keep your damned doors!" He said it under his breath, many times. Then he'd snap his fingers for Queenie, stride out, and hear behind him Louise's scornful voice: "No, Daddy! Don't call him! . . . No, Daddy! Don't . . ."

As if David could call him back. As if they still had any power over him—

"No, Daddy!"

All night the scene rattled in his head, in some strange area between dream and wakefulness. When morning came, he was exhausted, put his head under the pillow, and slept till noon.

He got up, made a sandwich, and hid in his room again. Gib was gardening, and anyone who passed without an obvious errand was apt to be drafted. In the next room he heard Julia moving, like an animal in an adjacent stall.

Chad couldn't stay still either. He paced and stretched, trying to make the feeling in his chest, the feeling like a hole, go away. On his desk was the book David had put into his hands, moments before everything blew up. Somehow it had made it all the way home with him, and now it gave Chad a little jolt, as if he'd discovered a bugging device, as if the book had given David the ability to listen to him here.

Automatically his hand went to his pocket. He was carrying a clicker, too, a body wire.

"No, Daddy! Don't call him!"

He knew this feeling: when he'd broken Helen's red glass candy dish and hadn't told; when he was four years old and he'd teased the old cat till she scratched him, and he'd told Mom he cut himself, and she couldn't figure out how.

But why should *he* feel guilty? It was them—

"Sky! *Sky!*" Gib screamed, and Chad's bones went liquid.

Julia thumped onto the landing, pounded downstairs. "Oh no! Oh my God!"

Chad went down the stairs hardly touching them, heading for the front door.

Gib burst in with Sky in his arms. Sky was half crying, scared. Mom came up the cellar stairs looking just as scared, and Gib said quietly, "Rabid coon. Out by the garden."

"Did it get near him? Sky, did you touch anything?"

"He was about fifteen feet away—"

"Where's Queenie?" Julia ran out onto the deck, and Chad followed. Old Yeller, he was thinking. He got rabies. He had to be shot.

"She's been vaccinated, right?"

"Kids, *don't*!"

The voices behind him only half made sense, and below Queenie circled the coon.

Chad knew at once that it wasn't normal, though it didn't foam at the mouth or rush madly. It just bumbled around. It was here in broad daylight where it shouldn't be, and it crept in slow, stupid circles. That was the extent of its madness: that, and the sick sheen in its eyes, opaque and greenish when it turned its head their way.

"Queenie!" Julia screamed. *"Queenie!"*

Queenie paid no attention. She darted at the coon, but halfheartedly, as if she sensed something wrong. She looked as if she wanted to be called off, but Julia's shrieks didn't penetrate. "You guys have pretty much burned that cue," David had said yesterday.

Chad pulled out his clicker, his stolen clicker. He ran down the deck stairs while Mom and Gib and Julia yelled, *"Chad!"*

He leaned over the railing halfway down and waited till Queenie's circling brought her to face him.

Click!

Queenie looked up, her big ears straight like funnels to catch the sound. Chad clicked again.

Queenie gave one quick, worried glance at the coon. Was this right? Then she came directly to Chad.

Click! Chad caught her around the neck. He rubbed her chest and whispered, "Good girl! Good Queenie!" He led her up the stairs and into the house, and while the rest of the family said, "Whew!" and "Wow, you got her!" and "Chad, don't you ever do that again!" he got out the hot dogs and gave her two.

Then he joined everyone else at the window. The coon

blundered against the wire mesh fence and huddled there. It must be hot all through; that must be what rabies felt like. Every cell must be burning.

"Poor thing," Mom said. They'd been afraid, but it was the one in trouble. In all its wandering, looking for ease, it had ended up here against their fence. If it would die, if it could only just die!

But it faltered on, slowly, bumping into the wire. Mom went to the phone. "Dad," she said in a moment, "we have a rabid coon here. Can you come down?"

Chad didn't want to look at the coon and couldn't stop watching. Only when he heard Jeep's truck did he go upstairs, sit on his bed, and plug his fingers into his ears so hard it hurt.

For a while nothing happened. What was taking Jeep so long? Maybe the coon wasn't . . . no, it *was* sick. So sick. With his lids squeezed shut, Chad saw the green glow of its eyes, burning inside, and nothing could put out—

The sound of the shot went through him, dense and blunt as the bullet itself. He kept his fingers in his ears a long time, but when he took them away, he heard a shovel striking into dirt.

Later, below him in the kitchen, Mom said, "We need a gun in this house. We shouldn't have to call my father every time something like this happens."

"This is the first time something like this ever has happened," Gib said. "I'm a child of the suburbs; I don't know how to shoot!"

"He never taught us girls, but shouldn't one of us know how? To protect our kids?"

"A gun in this house would *threaten* your kids, every

minute of every day. You've got a wild daughter, a depressed and withdrawn older son, and a little boy who's into something every minute. Do you *really* want a gun?"

You also have no doors, so maybe you should lower your voices when you talk about your children! Chad thought.

Mom said, "Oh, I know. But—"

"But a man's not a man if he can't shoot things!"

"That's silly, and you know it! But sometimes you have to, and we can't, and it makes me feel as if I'm not a grown-up. If we'd come along after Shep got hit, we'd have been helpless!"

Gib sighed, heavily enough to be heard all the way upstairs. "I know. Though what Chad's putting him through—"

Chad sat up on his bed. What *I'm* putting *him* through?

"What I love about your father," Gib said, "after his upbringing, all he's done, he's still—he's like a tree trunk. It looks dead, like it couldn't possibly be hurt, but nick it and it's full of sap."

"Mmm!" It was the sound of a hug. They were quiet for a moment. Then Mom said, "Should we get Chad into therapy?"

"I had therapy at his age," Gib said. "Know why? I was building space stations in my mind—every waking moment! But the therapist didn't want to hear that, so I made stuff up."

"What kind of stuff?"

"Let's just say it would have kept me from ever being drafted!"

"Chad's not building space stations."

"I have a lot of faith in Chad," Gib said. "This stuff he's doing with David Burton is making a difference."

You can say that again! Chad thought. They were observing him more closely than he'd realized.

And what did they know? Nothing!

Still, when he went downstairs for supper, he liked them, all of them, even Sky. Even Queenie. They were precious, though not perfect—mixed blessings, as Gib often said of Sky.

All weekend they were nice to one another.

C H A P T E R

16

MONDAY IT ALL went sour. At breakfast not one of his family seemed like any sort of blessing. Sky dribbled milk down his chin disgustingly, and Mom didn't seem to notice. Gib read the newspaper. He'd jogged to the bottom of the road for it in the loudest of his shirts and the shorts where the dye job divided exactly between the cheeks. Chad remembered making that pair. It had been a joke. He'd never expected anyone to wear them, let alone his father.

Julia was Julia. That was all it took.

This time last week he'd been heading down to his job. Done with that already, like a toy broken by Christmas afternoon.

He lingered at the table when the rest of them left, trying to do the newspaper crossword puzzle. None of the clues made sense. Mom came to put on the teakettle. "Hadn't you better get going, Chad?"

He shrugged and waited, determined to make her ask and have it out in the open.

"Chad? Is something wrong?"

That wasn't the question he wanted to answer. He shrugged again, but she didn't go on, and he finally said, "I'm not going."

"Why not?"

"I just decided not to."

"Decided not to? Chad, it's a job! You can't just decide not to show up!"

"Why not?"

"Why *not*? Because he's counting on you!" The kettle boiled. Mom switched it off and poured her cup of tea. "Did something happen down there that I should know about?"

Chad shook his head. It was a little hard to say, even to himself, what had happened. "Door," he wrote into an open four-letter slot, ruining the crossword.

"Then what *are* you going to do?" Mom asked. "Don't keep shrugging. I can't stand it!"

Chad couldn't help shrugging again. It was all he had in him to do.

"Chad, you can't just mope around for the next month! You aren't playing baseball; you have to do something!"

Chad's shoulders started to shrug again, all on their own. Mom's hand clapped onto his neck. Her fingernails touched him, not digging, but almost digging. *"Don't!"*

Then she snatched her hand away. "Oh my God, look at me!" She turned to the stove. He heard a little splash. *"Ow!* Ow!"

That was something, anyway.

. . .

The sunbeam slanted deeper into the empty kitchen.

"Want to play the ambush game?"

Chad bent over the ruined crossword. Sky circled him and hauled at his arms. "Play with me! Play with me! Please, please, *please!*"

"Chad, *play* with him!" Gib barked from the computer table in the corner.

"You can't *make* people play!" Chad muttered, under cover of "prettypretty*pretty*please!"

Gib looked up. "Wanna bet?"

For Gib he seemed dangerous, though thin and not very muscled, and with his long, meek ponytail hanging down his back. Something hard in Chad, something alarmingly independent of his normal self, considered. *Could* Gib make him?

His shoulders twitched in a shrug. He followed Sky out onto the deck, to the broken-legged plastic horses and the one-armed cowboy.

Sky sat down with the toys, in a tangle of deck furniture all on its sides, and picked up the blond horse. "We have to be really quiet," he said in a piercing whisper. "Here comes the bad guy riding down the canyon—"

"I don't see a bad guy!"

Sky looked at him as if he were an idiot. "Pre*tend!* Now you have to make the good guy ride." He pushed the handicapped cowboy into Chad's hands. "He wants to catch the bad guy and make him tell where the money's hid. Ride, ride, ride." Sky made a whispery sound that was supposed to be whistling.

Chad jumped the cowboy over the fallen chair back. He

kicked the cowboy's legs against Sky's horse and, accidentally, against Sky's brown, soft hand.

"*Ow!*"

Chad kept kicking with the cowboy, knocking the horse over. "Blam-blam—killed him *and* his horse! Game's over."

"*No!* That's not—"

"Game's *over!*" Chad got up and vanished around the corner, hearing Sky's roar behind him and his father's angry voice.

He headed up the road. Halfway he met Jeep and Helen driving down. So no one was at the farm.

No one was in the barn either, and he went inside it.

It was dark in there, after the bright outdoors. The scent of new hay pressed down, heavy and sweet. A year ago he and Jeep had spent an hour, on a morning just like this, checking the bales to see if any were overheating. Packed this close, hay that was a little too green could generate an awesome heat— enough to set the barn afire.

The bales were strewn askew on top, and loose flakes of hay lay on the barn floor. Jeep must have checked by himself this year.

Jeep's tools leaned against the wall. Here was the anvil; here were the chains; here was the gambrel-stick by which the butchered pig and steer were hung, year after year, splayed open to cool in the November air. Harnesses and horse collars gathered dust, and deep in one corner, dustiest of all, was Jeep's red goat cart. When Jeep was twelve and had moved in with a family that was kind as well as hardworking, he'd been given this cart. It was the ambition of his life at that time to own a goat and drive it.

He'd had to move on. Chad never knew why. The tales had come according to what the two of them were working on at the moment, so he'd never pieced together Jeep's growing up to make a full, real story. Somehow from that farm, Jeep had gone on to others, then to driving for a small trucking company at the age of fifteen, and then into the army, the war in Korea, and back here to marry Helen. After he bought this farm, he visited the kind family. The goat cart was still there, and someone remembered that it had been given to Jeep.

All it would take was a bale falling off the high stack, arcing inexplicably toward that corner. . . .

He couldn't quite do it. Not quite.

He went outside, to the pigpen. The pig got up when it saw him and came over with a friendly *oink*. It was pinkish white, with twinkling little eyes behind stubby lashes.

"You're meat!" Chad told it. "Dead meat! You've only got till fall. Don't you know that?"

The pig gave a rich grunt and pushed its flat nose at him. He picked a broad dandelion leaf. The pig smacked it down.

It glanced up at him again and then along the fence, communicating with its eyes the way Shep used to. There, between two posts, lay Jeep's flat stick for scratching pigs' backs, weathered silver-gray, the edges rubbed smooth against generations of bristles.

Chad felt his heart swell and heat. Without thinking, he opened the latch and pushed the gate back.

The pig squeezed through the opening. Its head was down now. It didn't have anything more to say to Chad, or he to it. He went out into the woods and spent a long time throwing sticks in above the waterfall and watching them be swept downstream.

C H A P T E R

17

THE PIG ENJOYED itself in Helen's beans and her dahlia
bed, and all week the rest of them heard about it. "Spend a little money, I told him, and build a proper pigpen, or at least
close the gate!"

Jeep didn't say much. The first time he saw Chad, afterward, he gave him a short, steady look from under his lowered
brows.

But Chad didn't see much of Jeep, or Helen, or anyone. He
spent the week walking every trail that crossed the hillside: the
old roads, where Jeep had logged when Mom and V were
children; the newer roads, where he got his firewood out now;
the back pasture, where the young stock used to summer,
grown up to juniper and rosebushes in the years since Jeep
had sold his dairy cows. Sometimes Chad managed to leave
Queenie behind. Sometimes she came with him. It didn't

matter. What mattered was pushing himself, making his legs hurt. Sometimes if he went fast and far enough, he'd notice suddenly that the bruised feeling in his chest was gone. Noticing was enough to make it come right back.

Another week began, Monday and then Tuesday passing slowly moment by moment, but swiftly, too, because it was already eleven days since Chad had quit.

Eleven days ago had still been July. Now it was August. At the end of August Louise would go.

And let her! Let her! But it seemed to Chad that he could feel her down the hill there. If he let himself forget for a moment, it was magical. She was there. He might meet her.

She might kill him.

But he couldn't stay away any longer. By secret paths he passed the white house, often several times a day. Once he saw Gib there, and for a few days afterward his parents stopped looking quite as anxiously at him.

Another day Jeep was there with a forked stick in his hands, dowsing the line of the water pipe. David looked impressed, though it wasn't that special. Several volunteer fire fighters could find underground water this way.

Louise was never outside.

Then one afternoon, when he crossed above the house on a worn deer trail, there she was. At first Chad didn't see her. His heart drummed hard and quick, though he didn't know why, as if someone else were beating it.

A sapling shape near the edge of the lawn lifted its arms in a graceful oval to frame a dark-haired head. Chad's heart broke into a gallop. This felt magical, dangerous, magical.

Now Louise dropped her arms disgustedly, shook them

out, and slowly lifted them again. Chad saw no difference, but she seemed satisfied. She drew herself up, rising onto her toes. She believed she was alone. I should go, Chad thought. But at that moment he saw the glint of chrome through the trees.

Jeep's truck. Always Jeep, prowling this road a dozen times a day. He pulled across the end of the green driveway and spoke to Louise out the window. She went toward him, and Malkin appeared from somewhere to follow her. Chad saw the white flash of Jeep's teeth. Jeep was handsome, even from this distance, and especially when he smiled. The teeth seemed like a flash of spirit, a true communication. The smile was what Jeep withheld. The smile was his power.

Louise went to work to make him smile again. She must have, because he did smile. She stepped closer to the truck.

"Don't!" The sound of his own voice startled Chad, made him notice himself, hidden on a deer trail above a lonely house. He'd become a Peeping Tom, the kind of guy of whom people say, afterward, "He was quiet, a loner. But I never thought he'd do anything like that!"

The harm he'd done was to himself. A door, he thought. What was so bad about a door?

All right, it wasn't just a door. It was Queenie. It was finding out how he'd been shaped to train her, to like her. David shouldn't have done it. He shouldn't.

The sound of laughter rose from the yard. Louise stepped back with Malkin in her arms, and the pickup rolled on down the hill, very quietly.

Chad drew a deep breath and held it. Louise had turned to face uphill. She stared straight at him, and Malkin did, too, ears and whiskers and the whole shape of his face funneling Chad in like a satellite dish.

Chad stood still. They couldn't see him. Could they?

After a minute Louise walked toward the house. Over her shoulder Malkin's round face turned, tracking Chad, homing in on him.

H E WOULDN'T SPY on them anymore. He'd stay away.

The trouble was he missed them, both of them. He even missed training Queenie. He missed doing something new and hard with his mind, and he missed wondering if he'd see Louise for a moment, if he'd think of something to say this time.

Thursday morning he filled his pockets with oyster crackers. "Let's go for a walk, Queenie."

Her eyes met his for an instant. *That's* what I want, Chad thought. "Sit" and "heel" and "come" were useful, but what he wanted was a dog that met his eyes.

So click her.

Too late. She stood ready to go, her nose an inch from the doorknob. Chad let her out and followed her golden tail down the driveway. He didn't want to train her to meet his eyes. He'd had that with Shep without ever trying.

Queenie paused at the bottom of the drive, looking back at him. Which way?

Uphill. Things being what they were. He angled his shoulders that way, and with something of a slump Queenie turned. She'd rather go to David's.

"Know what you mean," Chad said. She looked at him. His hand was in his pocket, his thumb was on the clicker. What the heck! He clicked and tossed her a cracker.

Fresh horse tracks marked the road. Big tracks. Rocky. Chad opened his senses wide, trying to drag in the scent of Louise's violet perfume. Nothing. The tracks might have been made this morning, or two hours ago, or fifteen minutes.

"What do you think?" Queenie looked back at him. *Click!* Cracker. And now, downhill, the quick rub-a-dub of galloping hooves. Chad's heart pounded.

But it wouldn't be Rocky, not coming that fast. Chad put a hand on Queenie's collar and stepped to the edge of the road. Tiger swooped around the corner, head high and pointed straight like a lance, Julia braced against the reins.

Tiger didn't seem to see Chad until he was right beside him. Then he made an explosive sideways leap. One hind foot plunged into the ditch opposite. A forefoot knuckled over. He nearly went down. Julia lurched onto his neck in a flapping of loosened rein.

Then Tiger scrambled up and on, Julia shouting, "Dammit, Chad!" They disappeared over the crest of the hill in a spatter of flying gravel.

"Jeez!" Queenie looked up at him. *Click!* "Excuse me for living!" He flipped her a cracker.

Queenie ignored it. A smile dawned in her eyes, warming them. She gave a little wag and a tiny, all-over wiggle and licked his hand. Then she capered up the road in front of him, front paws reaching high and prancy like a carousel pony's.

Chad stared after her. What did she mean? It seemed as if she'd said, Oh! I get it! I'll do that for free.

Could she mean that?

"Queenie?"

She looked back at him, and he crouched, arms wide. She came, looking unsure, and he grabbed her, ruffled her chest exuberantly till the corners of her mouth stretched in a grin. "Wait'll I tell David—"

You don't work for David anymore! his brain reminded him.

"Queenie? Do you think I'm an idiot?"

That dog smile again, warm and steady in the eyes. Maybe, it said. So what?

A few minutes later he heard a slow crunch of hoofbeats above him, and voices, and headed into the woods with Queenie. When he turned, he saw Louise's white-helmeted head, gliding downhill as if disembodied.

Only one head? He could hear Julia. She must be leading Tiger. Something must have happened.

"I'll be all right!" Louise's cold and colorless voice carried through the trees. What was going on? Chad nearly dislocated himself, standing on tiptoe to see better while keeping hold of Queenie's collar.

"God, I'm sorry!" Julia. She seemed to be walking between the horses, leading both. "He gets the bit in his teeth . . . Are you *sure* you're going to be all right?"

"Yes . . . I'm . . . fine."

Tiger must have galloped up behind Rocky and reminded him of his bucking days. Louise *was* hurt. Chad was sure.

"Come, Queenie!" He bounded downhill at a widening angle to the road, faster and more recklessly as he got out of earshot, dropping down steep slopes, crashing through brush. When he reached his lookout, they hadn't arrived yet.

He waited; it seemed like an hour. Finally the horses came into the yard. He heard Louise call, "Daddy!" but when David came out, Chad couldn't hear their voices. David hurried to Louise's side and helped her down. She tested her right leg, putting weight on, then a little more before she collapsed onto David's arm. He helped her into the house.

Numbly Chad watched Julia being pulled in opposite directions by the grazing horses, watched her watch the door.

He was supposed to hate Julia. She had taken Shep out with her and he'd been hit by the car. Now she'd hurt Louise, and Louise was a dancer. She couldn't afford to hurt her legs.

But Julia looked small down there, a huddled patch of too many colors, and she must feel terrible.

Chad didn't like knowing that. He didn't like caring.

Against his will he remembered when it was just the two of them, out on the swing set, playing in Jeep's barn. Julia did everything first because she was oldest, then helped him because he was little. They'd slid down the big rope in the haymow, and the bristles had pricked their tender palms. He'd cried, and Julia had taken him to the water tub and washed his hands. It hadn't helped, but she had done it.

David came out and took Rocky's reins. Tiger tossed his head and sidled his haunches and rushed off the moment Julia put foot to stirrup. She swung up, anyway, hard and lithe as a trick rider, her leg just crossing Tiger's back as he passed out of sight between the trees. David looked after her, shaking his head.

A deerfly stung Chad's neck. He swatted it, crushed one on Queenie's nose, and waited. David put Rocky in the pasture, helped Louise out to his car, and drove away.

Not till the next morning did Julia call to find out how Louise was doing. Chad lurked, listening, waiting, until finally he heard her dial.

"Hi. How's your leg? . . . Good. . . . Good. . . . Good." With each repetition Julia's voice warmed. Louise's must be warming, too, on the other end of the line.

Julia laughed. "Rice? What's that mean?" Pause. "Rest. Ice. Compression. Elevation. R I C E! So you're going to be okay?" Longer pause. "Good! Do you still feel like coming to my birthday party? Great! Friday evening around five. My little brother's dying to see you."

Chad's blood went hot, and then Julia said, "No, Sky! So how come Chad's not working for your dad anymore?" She listened. Chad's heart went *bom-bom-bom.* "Oh. Okay, I won't ask."

What had she said to Julia? What could she have said?

Anyway, she was coming. Chad had thought she would never step into this house again, and she was coming.

19

THROUGH THE NARROW slit between blanket and door-
frame Chad watched Louise come in. She limped a little. One
ankle, under green leggings, looked bulky.

Sky ran to hug her. "Lou-*weez*! Lou-weez! You didn't come
play with me!"

"I'm here now. Did you build the horse cave?"

"Yes, but you never came, and then it rained and Mom
brought the chairs in. I can build it again now."

"Now probably isn't a good time because it's Julia's party.
Did you help frost the cake?"

"Yes! I saved you a spoonful of frosting. It's in the 'frigera-
tor, in a yogurt cup. Here!"

Chad stepped back from his blanket. You saved her *frosting*?
Sky, boy, you're in a bad way!

He slid through the wall to look at himself in Julia's mirror.

The mustard had never quite come out of the one white T-shirt, or the ground-in hay chaff out of the other. His third shirt wasn't all it might be, and he'd dug out last year's BARRETT BASEBALL shirt. It was blue, faded French ultramarine, and it had shrunk, or he had grown, because it fitted close across his shoulders. He didn't look muscled, though. He looked . . . thin. His hair was short and light blond from sun, and he was tanned and . . . thin.

He went downstairs in his bare feet.

Louise leaned against the dishwasher, spooning her frosting out of a lemon yogurt cup. When Chad came in, her eyes made no change. She looked right through him, and the bottom of Chad's stomach rushed toward the floor.

But her face flushed, all the way to the forehead. She wasn't ignoring him, just pretending. He wasn't a dog to be fooled that way.

"Hi," he said.

She hesitated and said, "Hi." Her voice was colorless; that was pretend, too. Now if he could think what to say! It would help if he knew what he thought or what he wanted.

Meanwhile he could get a soda. He could go to the refrigerator, passing her, brushing her shirtsleeve with his elbow. . . . His heart banged so loudly he was afraid she'd hear it. He grabbed a soda and stepped away from her.

A car arrived. Queenie barked. Below waist level Sky gabbled about some game. Chad asked, "How's David?"

Louise flushed darker. "He's a little stuck, no thanks to you! He doesn't understand. He's a trainer, so he doesn't believe that some people are unimprovable jerks!"

Chad just stood while her words beat on him. Okay, he was grateful for any attention from her. He *was* a dog.

"It was just a stupid *door*!" she said. "You helped Daddy with the stove, and I thought you'd *like* it." He saw a shine of angry tears in her eyes.

"I'm going to have a door," Sky said. "It's going to have spikes like a castle door, and a moat—"

"Good!" Louise said. "I think *spikes* are a great idea!" She took Sky's hand and stalked toward the sliding glass door.

The unopened soda can was wet and slick, warm already. Chad put it back in the refrigerator and went out the front door. His mind felt perfectly blank. He had no plan, no idea what to do next.

V was climbing the stairs. She wore red today, a vibrant silky tunic. Julia hovered at her elbow. "Aunt V, I *really* need your help. Could you do a reading on Tiger? Because—"

V raised her chin so her profile looked cold and elegant. "You know I never give a reading without being compensated. In this culture nothing is valued that comes for free."

"I'll—"

V turned away, lips folded in the line that said she wouldn't speak for hours. Since V was beautiful, that line of her lips was beautiful, not sullen and childish. She nodded to Chad—he was included in the coldness—and went around the corner. "Oh! Hello, Louise!"

Who's withholding what? Where's the hoop?

David's mantra flashed through Chad's mind, and everything popped into focus.

V kept them on the hook with her blazing attention, with the power of *sometimes*. *Sometimes* she would look into your eyes in that intense way. *Sometimes* she seemed to know things about you that you only half suspected and nobody else had any idea of.

And sometimes not. Most times not, but did anyone remember that? Only a little bit, only in the apprehensive quickening of the heartbeat when she was near.

Louise refused to be caught. She stood looking almost rudely distant, till Sky led her away to the table.

Chad followed. He felt strange, dizzy almost. Everything was unnaturally clear, like waking after sickness, the morning when you're finally better, and weak, and famished. He perched on the deck railing near, but not too near, the picnic table and watched.

If you didn't listen, it was like a dance. Louise and Sky were partners. Jeep and Helen were partners, but Helen kept ushering other dancers up to Jeep, getting Gib or V or Julia to talk to him, standing back approvingly . . . while Julia tried to dance with V, or tried to butt in between Sky and Louise, and V tried to dance with Louise, and Louise politely ignored her.

On the edge of this circle of giving and withholding Mom juggled hamburgers, buns, ketchup, and salad. "Gib, I could use a hand here! V, do you think you could toss this salad?" At the moment Mom was the one Chad liked most, even more when she walked by and glared at him. Get off the railing! that look meant. Once she'd passed, he slid down, feeling grateful. She could have said it out loud. She could have embarrassed him severely. He tossed the salad since V showed no sign of doing it.

"These your tomatoes?" Jeep asked Gib when the salad was put on the table.

"These are them! I try to have tomatoes by Julia's birthday, but I don't always make it."

Jeep looked at him. You could reasonably conclude it was a curious look. Gib started to explain his techniques, and Helen smiled approvingly. For once Gib was talking about something that interested Jeep. She turned to V and fended her off from interrupting the men. The hamburgers sizzled, Mom took orders for cheese on top, and Chad sliced it.

"Thank you!" she said, sounding so surprised that Chad looked directly at her. It felt as if he hadn't done that in a long time. He made a face, half smile and half grimace, and she just stared, probably not knowing what to think. Chad couldn't have helped her out. He put the cheese on the burgers and listened to the background noise.

"Louise, look!" Sky kept insisting, and Julia would say, "So, Louise—" Both of them softly. *Both* of them!

"I think these are ready, Chad," Mom said. He held the platter for her and then put it on the table, between Jeep and Sky so he wouldn't brush Louise's shoulder. Having created a space there, he sat down, feeling her to his left like a radiating sun.

Queenie squeezed past his legs and lay under the table, pointing at him like an arrow. Chad bore down on the smile that wanted to break over his face. He cut a piece of hamburger with the edge of his fork. Looking straight ahead, showing, he hoped, no expression, he dropped the meat between Queenie's paws. He heard her snarfle and gulp. When he risked a glance again, she was lying with her chin just off the floor, aiming her eyes at him.

He couldn't afford to have V see this, but he couldn't afford not to respond either. This was the two-way street. He waited for a moment, shaping her to lie down longer. Queenie thumped her elbows on the deck, scrabbled her hind legs, and gave him a laughing, sassy look. He flipped her another piece of burger.

All right, he thought. All right. If I'm going to let my dog manipulate me, I could take a door from David and Louise.

There was no way to tell Louise. She wouldn't look.

Pia and Chess called midway through lunch, from horse camp. Julia looked happier when she came back out to open presents.

There was a tack shop gift certificate from Mom, and from Gib, the key to the car with the sapling through its bumper. "By the time you have your license it'll be running again." There was a shirt from Helen that Julia didn't like: neat and pale blue and girlie. From Jeep came a pair of earrings like little silver stirrups. "How did you *know*?" she asked, and Jeep just smiled.

Then she opened Chad's present. Chad looked toward the sliding door behind him as the paper ripped. Maybe he should vanish.

Too late. The paper was off, and Julia was flushing with pleasure. "Oh! Chad, thank you!"

"A horse model?" Mom kept herself from saying, Aren't you too old for horse models? but didn't keep the thought from being apparent. Maybe that was good because it cut off Julia's question. If she'd asked *him* how he knew, he'd have no good answer.

And if she asked him why? A range of answers was possible. I thought you wanted it. I thought it would embarrass you. I thought I'd be embarrassed if Louise knew I didn't get you anything—and that was truest. He'd biked to town for the present only after he'd known Louise was coming. He was happy to see Julia set the horse model beside her plate and open Louise's present.

She put aside the wrapping and flushed deeply. A clicker with a plastic coil so you could wear it on your wrist. A bag of horse treats. A booklet on clicker-training horses.

Julia sat red-faced and tongue-tied, frowning. Why? Chad wondered.

A frown started to gather on Louise's brow, too, that beautiful swirling frown that made it look as if she were too gentle for anger, though that wasn't true. She opened her mouth to say something, glancing swiftly at Chad as if he shared in Julia's offense.

The accident! Chad realized. Julia thinks—

"Can I see?" He reached across for the booklet, turning his head to look straight at Louise. She thinks it's an insult! he thought at her, making a face.

Louise settled back in her chair, angry and bewildered.

"Thank you," Julia said stiffly and reached for the envelope from V. She opened it and turned to V. "But you said—"

"Happy birthday, Julia!" V said. "Of *course* I'll give you a reading. We can do it right now."

"*Cake*, V!" Mom said.

But V took Julia's hand and drew her toward the deck railing. Now she was looking at Julia, giving her the ultimate in attention. Julia, embarrassed, glanced back toward the picnic table.

Poor Julia! Chad thought. What a rotten birthday!

She deserved it. She took Shep with her—

But that felt thin suddenly, like a movie seen once too often. Shep was gone, and here inside him, and maybe somewhere else, too, maybe out there in the ether where V claimed to communicate. Right here, right now Chad could give Julia something that mattered: the chance not to spoil things with Louise.

He looked over Sky's bobbing blond head and said, "She thinks it was an insult. Because of your accident. She thinks you're telling her to train her damned horse already!"

Louise's jaw dropped. "*Oh!* Oh! I never met a family it was so hard to be nice to!"

She wouldn't give up being mad at him. Chad sat back in his chair and then thought, What the heck!

"Is David home tomorrow?" he asked.

"He's always home!" She made that Chad's fault. All right, she hated him. At least she was paying attention.

"Tell him I'll be down."

20

HE PUT ON the BARRETT BASEBALL shirt again. It smelled the tiniest bit, but Louise wasn't coming within smelling distance! His jeans, he discovered, had a chocolate ice-cream drip on one thigh, from yesterday's party. He scrubbed it off with a washcloth, leaving a large wet patch. But his other jeans were even worse, and anyway, the first time she'd seen him he hadn't had any shirt on at all, and his jeans had been dark with hay grime.

He collected the clicker and *Don't Shoot the Dog!* It was unfortunate that his parents, working at the long table, saw him leave with Queenie. They didn't comment. Mom smiled, though, and Chad felt himself turn red. It would have been better to have kept this a secret, because maybe nothing would come of it. Maybe his job was finished, anyway.

Partway down the road, nearer his house than the Burtons',

a figure stood up from the stone wall as he drew near. Chad was almost not surprised. He'd almost known she'd be there.

She wore leggings and a green tunic and would have looked like Robin Hood except for the thick-soled, cushiony sneakers. She barely limped as she stepped into the road.

Chad thought he would make a joke: Is this a stickup? Something like that. But his voice caught in his throat. She swung in to walk beside him, and for a minute he thought she wasn't going to speak either.

"I didn't tell Daddy you were coming," she said abruptly. "I wasn't sure you would."

Still mad. Scary, Chad had to admit. Nonetheless it lit a tiny spark of cheer in him. He didn't know why.

Louise said, "All right! I get how I insulted your sister. Now, how about you?"

Chad opened his mouth and closed it again.

"Doors? You've got a thing about doors?" She was getting angrier.

Chad's voice almost stuck, but he pushed it. "You were . . . conditioning me. You both were."

Louise whirled to face him, and one knee collapsed. "*Ow!* Damn! I was *thanking* you! I thought I'd found the perfect thing you needed, and you threw everything back in our faces!"

Chad could only shake his head, not denying it, just overwhelmed. Yes, he'd done that. He remembered feeling like Jeep as he walked out. Feeling like a man . . . She was frowning at him. He had to say something. "It made sense at the time." Then in all honesty he had to add, "I think."

That surprised an angry little laugh out of Louise. "I'd love to know what kind of sense you think it made!"

"It was— Well, look! I *told* him I didn't want to train Queenie. He knew, and there I was doing it anyway! I got suckered into it. 'I'll just demonstrate this point, I'll just demonstrate that point,' and look at her!"

Queenie had turned her face up at his rising voice. Her eyes looked concerned. He gave her a quick pat.

"He shouldn't have done that," Louise said, more quietly. "But I know why he did."

"Why?"

"Because—" She paused to think. She was forgetting to be mad. Chad felt a bit angry himself now, as if her cloud of emotion had drifted sideways onto him. "Number one, he thought you'd be better off if you liked her."

"That was none of his business."

"Maybe. But if you can help people—"

"You should wait till they *want* help!" Chad said.

Louise's eyebrows knitted again. "All right! The other reason is that you could help him. You and Queenie were perfect. Neither of you knew a thing about training. You were just what he needed."

Chad felt his face go hot. He walked along looking at his feet. Valuable because he didn't know anything. Well, he'd known that. But he'd thought there was something special about him, too. Those sharp, surprised looks David and Louise used to give him, as if he'd just said something brilliant . . .

"He likes you," Louise said, more gently. "He's going to be so alone after I go."

Chad's spirits sank deeper. That was how he mattered to Louise. He could fill the gap in David's life. Why didn't she get her father a dog? It would be a lot easier!

His voice came huskily, saying something he didn't want to say, but why not? How much worse could things get? "I thought you were going to be there. At least sometimes."

Louise's white sneakers stopped walking. Chad made himself look up, and up, till he met her eyes.

They were bright and challenging, and she was smiling, too, in a way that made him feel every month and week and hour of the year's difference in their ages. At the same time a trickle of excitement started to run deep in his body.

"Are you telling me?" she said. "Are you . . . telling me—"

Chad felt like Tarzan, swinging on a vine out over an abyss. What was down there? It didn't matter. He let go. "I'm telling you."

Louise's eyes sparkled. She swung around to start walking again, and the corner of her mouth made a small, secret movement. "Interesting," she said. "In-ter-est-ing. Now let me tell you a few things! Number one, I'm older than you!"

"And taller!"

"Number two, I'm going away."

The fizz in Chad's blood couldn't be flattened out, even by this. "You'll be back," he said. "Sometimes."

"Number three," Louise said, "Daddy *made* me leave, so you wouldn't be embarrassed."

"*Embarrassed!* I wouldn't have been embarrassed!"

"Well, you were! Anytime I was around, you were too embarrassed even to think!"

That wasn't embarrassment, Chad wanted to say. But that might not be a good idea.

"Anyway, I knew you were with Daddy, and it was my chance to get out for a while. I don't like him to be alone right now. And I did see you, every day. Sometimes twice!"

She waited for Chad to acknowledge that, and he nodded. "Besides, I like your little brother."

"He's a pain."

"He's a pain because you're trying to ignore him, just the way you were trying to ignore Queenie. And *that's* none of *my* business! Just like the door was none of my business. Gonna take your marbles and go home?"

Chad felt his heart beat in his chest, high and thin and giddy. He said, "Don't have enough left to make it worthwhile."

Louise laughed out loud and took his arm for a second, just a little squeeze. It left Chad completely disorganized, unable to listen to what she was saying. She was a dancer. She touched people all the time. It didn't mean—

"You have to *talk* to Daddy," she was saying. "If you just walk back in and don't say anything, he won't either. Daddy doesn't really believe in words."

Over his head again—what a beautiful feeling! Go ahead, confuse me more! She'd dropped her hand, but she walked so close his arm hairs prickled straight out toward her.

"I keep telling him," she said. "Words *are* behavior! Human behavior. That doesn't mean they aren't valid."

"I never know what you're talking about!" Chad said, and a loopy-feeling grin spread across his face. Louise smiled, too, and right then Chad decided he would become a painter. If there were things in the world as beautiful as Louise's smile, he had to do something about them.

CHAPTER

21

Now what? Everything was changed yet not changed. It was the same but carbonated. The same but painted over with a golden glaze. A few more yards down the road, laughing without anything to laugh at . . .

In David's driveway stood a gleaming blue VW Beetle.

Louise stopped short. "What?"

She looked at Chad, looked *down* at him. Okay, I can live with that, Chad was thinking. I'll grow.

"No," Louise said. "No." Swiftly she went ahead of Chad, into the house.

". . . telephone," V was saying, in the kitchen. "People call and tell me the animal's name, describe the problem, and I get in touch with the animal and call them back."

"Really?" David's voice sounded so neutral it was almost a

joke. Louise walked into the kitchen. Chad followed, and David's face lit up.

"*Chad!* I was afraid—" He broke off and just smiled, looking intensely relieved.

"Hello, Chad, Louise." V wasn't enchanted to see them. A plastic container rested on the table. Through the translucent sides Chad saw her justly famous macadamia-nut cookies. David opened the container and offered it around.

"These are the best," Chad said.

Louise took a bite, and her eyebrows shot up. "Wow!"

Queenie sat at Chad and then lay down as if for extra emphasis. She knew these cookies, too.

Chad broke her off a corner and felt a reaction from V. He looked up, his face heating.

V's mouth opened, as if to speak. Then she met his eyes and smiled, a tiny, scrunched-up smile that wrinkled her nose. Her freckles stood out for a moment, and she looked like a farm girl, not a psychic beauty. Oh! I *like* V! Chad thought.

She looked away from him quickly and said to David, "You must have work to do. I'll go. I need to phone a client, anyway."

David had half risen to see her to the door, but this seemed to catch him. He frowned at V. "What makes you believe you actually contact these animals?"

"Results," V said. "I hear remarkable stories—"

"I'll bet! But what I mean is . . . don't you think you're making it up? You can say anything you want! The animal can't contradict you. It's like a child playing with a doll, making up a story. Anyway, that's what it seems like to me. Do you understand that?"

For some reason this speech, which should have made

Louise glad and V angry, had the opposite effect on both. Louise flushed and frowned, and V kept smiling. "I give myself permission to believe what I see. I give myself permission to learn and improve."

When she said things like that, Chad always wondered: What if it was true? What if V could read minds, and contact spirits, and understand dreams?

He remembered his dream about Shep, the one so real he woke up happy, though he knew Shep was dead. The strong nudge of the dog's nose under his hand; he was sure he'd really felt that. Then Shep had bounded off joyously, never looking back. Movin' on, was the message Chad had gotten. No regrets . . .

V said, "We manifest what we concentrate on. There are rules; there's a science. You need to ask the universe questions it can answer yes to."

David's head jerked slightly. "Go on!"

"Classic example: A mother prays for her sick child. 'Don't die, don't let her die.' But the universe doesn't hear negatives. It doesn't hear 'don't.' The universe hears 'Die. Let her die.' "

David sat up straight. "By *universe* I take you to mean God, and I wholeheartedly reject a God who would be that small-minded. But there *is* evidence that the unconcious mind works the way you've described, and I'd like to discuss that with you. Not now, because Chad and I have work to do, but sometime. Will you leave me your phone number?"

V's cheeks were very pink, her eyes bright. She pulled the pad of paper on the table toward her and scribbled her number.

"You're on to something," David said. "What you've made of it is unmitigated crap, but the underlying idea interests me."

V just smiled, a peculiar, tense smile, head tilted a little. David had been pretty insulting, but V was pleased, as if everything up till then had been insulation and they'd finally touched the live wire.

Politely David followed her to the door, and Louise reached for another cookie. "These were a big mistake. Daddy *hates* sweet things."

"I'll tell her that," Chad said.

Louise frowned. "I'm *not* letting Daddy get scooped up on the rebound! Especially by somebody like your aunt!"

"Taste her pot roast before you make up your mind!"

Louise's mouth dropped open. "You're teasing me, aren't you? You little *twerp!*" Chad didn't care so much for the "little," but he liked the smile.

Then David was back. "Chad! I'm so sorry!" He took Chad's hand in a quick shake.

"So you know?" Louise said. "You know what you did?"

"Oh, I know," David said. "Chad, you told me you didn't want to train Queenie and I . . . interfered. I had no right."

Chad opened his mouth and didn't know what to say. Was he supposed to agree?

"She's a great dog," David said, "and at first I just wanted to get her into better hands. Then I saw that you could *be* those hands—but no excuses. It's an old temptation with me, one I thought I'd gotten over, but I'm a little off-balance right—"

"Daddy? Shh. Let Chad say something now."

Chad said, "Uh," and took a deep breath. "It's all right, I guess. I mean, can I have my job back?"

"Yes! God, yes! We can get a goat, a goat would be ideal—"

"Queenie's fine," Chad said. Queenie, sniffing at the base

of the sink for crumbs, lifted her head, and looked across the room at him. "I mean, it worked. I like her now."

David sat down with something of a thump and closed his eyes. After a moment he said quietly, "Good."

"She's a great dog," Louise said. "Chad was always going to like her someday."

Chad didn't think that was true. The hardness in him might never have changed. He'd held out against Queenie for months; he might have held out forever. David had reshaped him into someone who could no longer do that.

"Can you change anything?" he asked David. "I mean—"

David looked at him for a long moment. "You mean, do I use this often on my fellow human beings?"

"Yes."

"All the time," David said. "Not on purpose mostly. It's who I am now. The way I look at people has changed at a basic level; the way I respond has changed. I . . . look for what I like. I try to make it happen again. Sometimes . . . I get carried away."

"You said once this would change the world."

"I believe it will. We focus on what annoys us and ignore everything else. In the new culture we'll focus on positive change and be quick to help it along because that works. That creates a better life. So yes, I can change a lot. On the other hand, could I save my marriage? No."

"You made things better," Louise said. "You made things a lot less crazy!"

David said, "I raised a very nice daughter. That's what I did."

Have *I* changed? Chad wondered. Other than liking Queenie? Or was liking Queenie part of something bigger? It might be. The world seemed fluid to him, as if the old boundaries were not really boundaries, as if the limits and the laws were only veils. But what did that mean, really? What should he do?

David said, "You kids are being shaped every day. Adults are trying to mold you into what they like. I want you to understand that, so you can be an equal. Anyone who's shaping you can be shaped by you."

"Like land and water," Louise said.

The waterfall, Chad thought, the water wearing away the stone, the stone pouring the water onto the rock below, where it dug out a pool, where the rock dammed it, where it eroded the lip of the dam. Rock and water were equals, though the water was weak and slipped away, and the rock was hard and constant.

"Enough philosophy," David said. "Do you feel like working? If I can remember what we do next?"

"Yes." That was exactly what he did feel like: working, letting his mind slip along the cool channels of observation and choice.

"What do you want to do with her?"

Chad didn't know. What did you do with a dog besides hang out? "What do you need me to do?"

Louise slipped out of the room. A moment later Chad heard music come on in another part of the house. "Easy, boy!" it said to him. "I haven't gone anywhere."

David said, "Well . . . I guess we could start with targeting. You can go on to almost anything from there."

So they spent a while—twenty minutes at most—teaching Queenie to touch the end of a dowel with her nose. Of the three of them, she was the only one not rattled, not a little shy. By the end of the session Chad was already varying the reinforcement, withholding the click until she touched two or three times.

"She's a smart dog," David said. "You know that, don't you?"

"She's not bad," Chad said. It was still a little hard for him to admit that.

Louise poked her head into the kitchen. She gave Chad a direct, clear-eyed smile. "By the way, is it all right now to give you a door?"

David gave him doors for Sky and Julia as well, and Gib brought them home in the van. "Comes a time when a guy needs a door," he said to Chad. Chad thought they all had needed doors for a long time.

He'd imagined hanging them himself, but it turned out he didn't know how. Gib did, almost without thinking, and when Chad's door was a little too big, he shaved off the excess with a plane. That's right, Chad thought. Gib had built this house. Jeep hadn't done that. He hadn't built anything up at the farm. House and barn had already been there.

When Gib finished with the doors, Chad showed him the gaps in the walls.

"I'd forgotten about those," Gib said. "Real sieve up here, isn't it?" He looked around Chad's room, taking the measure of it and maybe of the person who'd shaped it. Chad looked at it, too; it felt as if he hadn't seen it, his own room, in a long time. Those paintings looked young to him. He thought he could do better.

Sky put his head through the gap. His face was red and puckered, and he looked as if he were about to cry. "I don't *like* my door!"

"Why not, buddy?" Gib asked.

Sky screwed his face up tighter and rubbed his eye with the heel of his hand. He didn't answer.

Chad knew. That made a warm, light feeling flow out of him. Everything was like that today, golden and glowing as if the air were ginger ale. He loved his own door, as creamy blank as a piece of hot-pressed paper, but Sky had wanted a moat, a drawbridge.

"Don't worry," he told Sky. "You're going to have the door of your dreams!"

CHAPTER

22

IT DIDN'T HAPPEN fast. First Chad had to draw a castle gate and courtyard on the outside of the door, a castle gate and landscape on the inside. The technical problems of perspective and illusion had been solved by medieval painters centuries ago, but that didn't make it easy. He'd been right, though; his drawing had actually improved. Maybe his color control had, too. As he drew on the pale door, his mind leaped ahead, trying to extract the greatest possible brilliance from his poster paints.

The next morning Louise limped up the hill to play with Sky. At noon, when Chad and Queenie walked home—Queenie knew the word *touch* now—Jeep's truck went down past them. Sky waved out the window. Chad hurried, but Louise was waiting out on the deck with her feet up.

"Daddy's coming to get me. I'm not up to walking both ways."

She could have gotten a ride home with Jeep, but she hadn't.

"Sky showed me his door," she said. "I didn't know you painted."

Chad looked down, shrugging. "We'll see. He wants a knight, a dragon, and a dog on it. *And* a beautiful lady!"

"Cool!"

"Actually," Chad said, "he wants you."

Louise looked directly at him. Her eyes were wide and clear and steady. After a moment she said, "He does, does he? Inside the door or out?"

"Uh, both. Both, actually. So . . . would you be willing to . . . pose for me?"

She considered him, looking cool and self-contained, though bright color stained her cheeks in triangles. She blushed exactly the way her father did. "Maybe," she said at last, firmly. "Let me see what you do with the door first, and then . . . maybe."

So the door was a test. Chad threw himself into painting: castle and landscape and dragon scales and dog—a golden dog with a plumy tail because gold showed up bright against the grass. As he worked, thoughts tumbled through his mind: complementary colors, and Louise, and Queenie.

Queenie seemed like a queen now, like someone you went to for very important favors. He wondered if she thought of him as someone who could grant favors, too, and if she had any idea that things had changed. Did she remember that a few weeks ago everybody had just yelled at her? Did she feel any dislocation because, out of the blue, people like himself and David had started applauding certain actions, started feeding her cues so she could get applause again? A person might conceivably be weirded-out by this change of tactics. Queenie just seemed waggy and content.

The brush stroked across the surface of the door. The colors brightened and deepened. The dog stood out more and more solidly, and the blank place stood out, too, a white place with ragged edges of paint where the beautiful lady would go—if this was enough to persuade her.

On the third day Louise looked at the door and said, "All right."

The next day she brought a long dress, as requested. To Chad's delight, it was a deep ruby red. He hadn't known what color he needed to complete the picture, but red was perfect. The dress was long-sleeved and hot; he brought her chair around to the shady end of the deck.

"So what am I doing in this picture?" Louise asked. "Waiting around for the knight to rescue me?"

A sharpness in her voice warned Chad. He said, "Maybe you're waiting around to rescue him!"

That made her laugh and relax a little, but Chad couldn't relax. He could hardly look at her, let alone draw. The first sketches were angular and lopsided and awful.

Maybe it was the pencil: too hard, too pointed. He switched to vine charcoal, pushing up and up the page in free, branchy swoops. Strokes for nose and mouth and chin; in one picture they were just the right strokes, short, beautiful lines that said "Louise."

"Your grandfather took Sky to lunch again," Louise said. "I thought that was nice, taking your grandson on a lunch date."

Keep talking, Chad thought. It freed her neck; it freed his

hand. "It is nice," he said, and the whole experience of lunch in town with Jeep flooded into his mind: the counter in the general store, the high stools and the odd-tasting water in thick plastic glasses, the BLT that squirted down your chin. Jeep. Good for Sky, and good that it was now, just when Chad most needed to be free of him.

Say something more, he thought at Louise. He couldn't talk and draw at the same time, not the kind of talking in which you think about what you're saying. He could throw out random comments or respond to them, but it felt like someone else speaking, as if there were three of them here, not two.

Fortunately Louise wanted to talk, about David mostly. They were creating a new life together, discovering new likes and new customs. She saw her father as fragile, needing constant care. "After the divorce I had to *train* him to cheer up. Everything he taught me about seeing what's positive—he didn't use it on himself. I had to show him: 'Look, you can read the paper at breakfast! Look, today no one will criticize you!' "

That might not make up for losing your wife, Chad thought. He stroked the charcoal across the paper, feeling out the dip in Louise's collarbone.

"I told him," Louise said, " 'The glass isn't half empty; it's half full.' "

"It's both, really," Chad said. "Has to be."

Louise swiveled to stare at him, ruining the pose. "That's what Daddy said!"

The charcoal made a lightning flash down the paper, catching the new position. "And what did you say back?"

"I said, 'You're right! Is the glass half full or half empty? That's not the question!' "

"What is the question?"

"Will you reach for the glass? Will you drink the water?"

The backs of Chad's eyeballs prickled. Will you drink the water?

I will, he wanted to say. But was that true? Was he the kind of person who reached for the glass? Or did he stand back, with arms folded and lips closed?

"Can I stand up now?" Louise stretched and came over to look at the sketch pad. "Oh!"

Chad thought even the back of his neck must be brick red. Now she was seeing what he saw when he looked at her.

"On the door it'll be mostly dress," he said. He'd be walking by that door several times a day, as she knew full well. He wasn't going to put an awkward, botched portrait there, and he wouldn't put up anything that would seem too intimate. It would be just a suggestion, just enough to say "Louise" to him. He didn't know how to put that into words.

"Well," Louise said, "tomorrow can we go for a walk? Because I need to start using this ankle. I was hoping you'd show me some of the trails."

She met him and Queenie on the road at noontime, wearing black shoes with high, thick soles. "They lace up tight," she said, seeing him look. "They support my ankle."

They appeared dangerous to Chad and made her two unnecessary inches taller. He chose the easiest trail he knew.

The next day she wore sneakers, but she still seemed taller. This time it was the hair, spiked nearly straight.

"Wouldn't you rather be able to wear a hat?"

Louise sparkled her eyes at him. "No! I don't want a hat!"

She wanted to be taller. She was making him safe to hang out with. Short, young, safe.

I'll take it! Chad thought. It's a start.

David had appointments that afternoon, so Louise wasn't in a rush to get back. Chad showed her the waterfall.

It was astonishingly cool there. A breeze off the falling water turned the hollow into a refrigerator. Louise looked for a long time, really seeing it, as Chad had wanted. He thought about saying how the stone shaped the water, how the water shaped the stone. But it was either obvious or too complex, and he didn't.

They sat on rocks by the edge of the pool, and Queenie waded into it to lap from the middle. Louise took off her sneaker and tenderly unwrapped her ankle. She sank it into the water with a sigh. "This is the one thing I wish hadn't happened this summer. School's already going to be hard enough."

"But you're looking forward to it, right? I mean, you're going to be a dancer."

Louise shook her head. "I'm not good enough, and I'm probably not driven enough. I could never make myself throw up, for anything!"

"Should you?"

"If I was serious about dance, I should think I'm fat. Even though I'm not. I should care that much."

"That's crazy!"

"I should be crazy. I should be sad that I'm *not* crazy! I think it's going to be an awful lot of work for someone who isn't crazy. I think I'm going to find out that lunacy is required."

"So . . . ?"

"I do love dance. I love how it looks. I love being *able* to. And leotards! I love leotards!" She was laughing. "It's a little girl thing. Oh well! An arts high school should be interesting."

"Yeah," Chad said glumly. Guys who could lift her with one hand, he was thinking. Guys who could paint like Michelangelo. Not in a million years was she going to remember her father's wimpy little research assistant. He stretched out an arm to snag Queenie as she passed, and pulled her close. "You'll be with your mother, anyway."

She made a face. "I'm a daddy's girl. But Mum's okay, as long as they aren't together."

It was none of his business, but Chad had to ask. "What happened with them?"

Louise hugged her knee, and rested her cheek on it. "Okay, what *I* think? I think his being a dog trainer was marginal for her, maybe right from the start, but lately for sure. But at least he was a *star* dog trainer. You saw his video, right?"

"He hates his video."

Louise nodded. The motion shivered the surface of the water. "He stopped being a drill sergeant and became Doctor Dolittle. But Mum didn't want to be married to Doctor Dolittle. So she took him to the cleaners in the good old-fashioned way and moved to New York. She even got our dog."

"How come she didn't get you?"

"She got most of me!" Louise said. "She got the school year!"

Dumb question, Chad thought. Sad answer.

Louise wrapped her ankle again, put on her sneaker, and they started across the hillside. To keep her interested, Chad was prepared to give away all his secrets. What he had left was the lookout point from which he'd watched her. After that he'd just have to think of something. Or she would.

They came to the lower edge of Jeep's hayfield. The green expanse opened before them, brilliant after the deep woods. Here they'd seen the fox, the day of that awful picnic.

Chad was about to remind Louise when, far up the hillside, he saw the tiny figure of a horse and rider. Julia's bright tie-dye was dimmed by distance into a sort of camouflage. Tiger's chestnut coat flamed against the green.

What were they doing? Around, around, around. Tiger's neck was high; his steps were short and mincing. Chad saw him shake his head, shorthand for what he really wanted to do.

At his side Queenie whined, and Chad put a hand on her neck.

Then Julia jerked on one rein, yelling. She jumped off. She slapped Tiger's neck, and the sound rang down the hillside. "I'd like to *kill* you!" The voice was small with distance and thick with sobs. "I'd like to sell you for *dog meat*!" Jerk! Slap!

Chad went hot all over. His heart seemed to sink through his body. He didn't want to look at Louise; he wanted to evaporate.

But he did look. Louise was—what? Shocked? Her mouth opened as if to speak, and tears sprang up in her eyes, drained back.

"Oh no!" she said suddenly, looking up toward the barn.

Jeep came running. Actually running. That was something Chad had never seen off the baseball diamond. Jeep's leather work boots sprang over the mown grass, never stumbling. He came swiftly, like a skipping boulder. Tiger backed away, shaking his head. Julia stood motionless, staring the way Chad was staring.

Jeep grabbed them. One hand wrapped into the cheekpiece of the bridle, dragging Tiger's head down. The other seized Julia's upper arm. He shook her. Her braid flapped twice. Now Jeep was yelling right into her face; his voice was deep, and his words were unclear. Julia crumpled, melting out of his hand into the grass.

Jeep turned from her and led Tiger up the hill. The horse's tail cringed into his haunches. Jeep stumbled once or twice, a short-legged man, seventy years old. All the way up the hill he marched, nonetheless, and disappeared into the barn.

Julia never moved, just lay where she was like a heap of laundry.

"We have to go to her," Louise whispered. There were streaks of white under her eyes, and she looked frightened.

Chad nodded. He didn't want to go anywhere near Julia, or Jeep, or Tiger. But Louise was right. They did have to. They crossed through the gap in the stone wall and started up the field.

They began to hear the low, heavy sound of crying. It made Chad sweat with embarrassment. She was groaning from deep inside, and he remembered how that felt, as if you had too much pain to keep in, as if you had to give birth to it, heave it out of yourself, and your throat was nearly too small. They shouldn't be here. When he'd cried like that, for Shep, he'd been deep in the woods, where no one could hear.

But Louise dropped to her knees beside Julia and put a hand on her back. Julia's body jerked. "It's Louise. And Chad."

Julia wrapped her arm around her head and pushed her face deeper into the grass. Even now she couldn't seem to catch the groans. Louise sat rubbing her back while the sounds slowly ran down. Chad stood a few feet away, smoothing one of Queenie's silky ears over and over between his fingers.

After a while Julia was quiet, just lying there. A change came in her breathing. She was starting to think, maybe come up with some story. Chad wasn't sure he could take that. He said, "We saw."

Julia stopped breathing, for what seemed like a long time. She didn't raise her head. After a while her voice came low and slow out of the grass.

"I hate myself. I hate myself. I can't do it. He should never, never have given me a horse to train. I don't know how. I don't know how. I—"

"Learn!" The harsh sound of Louise's voice made Chad jump. "You think you should automatically know how to train a horse? Were you supposed to be *born* knowing?"

Julia raised her head. Her face was pale and blotched and wet. "I try. I read my books—"

"I've seen your books! You're trying to read Shakespeare, for God's sake, without even knowing the alphabet!"

Julia didn't move or blink.

"Look, it's not your fault!" Louise said. "There are rules, they're simple, and you can do everything with them. You don't have to be a saint, and you don't have to be a horse whisperer, and you don't, for God's sake, need a psychic reading! You just have to learn the rules. Ask Daddy—"

"No!"

"Yes!" Louise said. "Yes!" She bent forward to look into Julia's eyes. Chad was outside the circle they made, standing while they were down in the grass, awkward while they were perfectly unselfconscious. Louise stared gently, fiercely at Julia.

At last Julia stirred, with a look of hope, and then her face crumpled again, and she dropped her head onto her arm. "Jeep's going to sell him."

Jeep. *Jeep.* Heat mushroomed through the core of Chad's body, swift and smooth.

"He won't do that," Louise said.

Julia said, "He will. He will. He can't stand cruelty to animals—"

"He *shoots* animals!"

The words ripped at Chad's throat. Louise started and looked up at him. Then she drew a deep breath. "He won't, once he knows you're getting help. I'll have Daddy talk to him."

Julia said, "The auction is tomorrow."

Yes, auctions were on Saturdays. Jeep always left early, his truck rolling past the house before it was light.

Louise said, "I'll talk to Daddy the minute he gets home." Jeep and what he would do weren't real to her. She thought she could brush it all away.

Chad drew a deep, openmouthed breath. Things seemed unusually vivid, as if an electric shock had cleared all his channels. Afternoon shadows streaked across the green and golden grass. Swallows dived. Chad could see the tiny insects they snatched from the air. Off in the woods a hermit thrush began her evening song.

No time. Louise would have trouble persuading David. He'd already made one mistake with their family. He didn't like Julia; he'd no sooner met her and Tiger there beside the moving van than he'd sent them away. It would take Louise awhile to bring him around, and by then it would be too late.

But Louise didn't know that. "You can't just lie here," she said to Julia. "Come to the brook, and wash your face. It'll be all right." She put her arm around Julia, lifting her. Julia went along passively, and Chad was left with the patch of crushed grass, the neon-bright helmet.

He picked it up. The padding was wet with Julia's sweat. He followed them to the brook. Louise patted Julia's face with a dampened tissue, as if they were best friends. Chad said, "I'll take this home." Louise nodded without looking.

Fine. She would do what she was doing. He knew what he had to do.

CHAPTER

23

THE DOOR WAS an unexpected handicap. Chad had to keep
opening it to hear when everyone fell asleep. Before, he'd
have known just lying on his bed.

Sky ran down about ten o'clock. Gib picked him up off the
floor and carried him upstairs.

Light shone from under Julia's door for a while longer,
then went out. Chad listened, pressing his ear to the wall.
Usually Julia tossed and turned, as the energy of her body
resisted sleep. Tonight she lay dead still. Chad knew that stillness: despair on top of you like a rock. Julia didn't believe in
David's help either.

After her light had gone out, he waited on the landing for a
long time, listening to the murmur behind Mom and Gib's
curtain. They knew something was wrong with Julia, so
wrong they didn't dare dig it out of her. Jeep hadn't called to

tell them. Apparently he didn't plan to; he'd just load Tiger at dawn and drive away.

The voices quieted. The glow of light from under their curtain vanished. About fifteen minutes later came a snore.

He waited a few minutes longer, then walked along the landing. His bare feet made no sound. Down the stairs, skipping the step that squeaked.

On the couch Queenie raised her head.

Chad glided past her through the dimly moonlit living room. He opened the front door. Queenie's claws scrabbled on the floor.

"No!" Chad whispered. He slipped through the door and closed it quickly. Immediately came Queenie's whine.

"*Shh!*" He opened the door again. Queenie came out and *thump-clatter, thump-clatter*ed down the stairs. Chad waited for his mother's voice.

Nothing.

He eased down the deck stairs and sat on the bottom step to put on his sneakers. Queenie stood nearly out of sight in the darkness. "What am I going to do with you?" Chad whispered. Clearly he couldn't leave her; she'd wake everyone up. If he took her—

Off to the east came the eerie wail of coyotes, maybe one, maybe ten.

Wouldn't hurt to have Queenie along.

He picked up his flashlight and made his way to the barn, felt along the pegs. No halter. Where could Julia have left it? He didn't want to turn the light on and spoil his night vision, but at last he had to. A rope was tied to the hitching ring, and the halter dangled from it with no horse inside. He untied the rope and slung it and the halter over his shoulder.

Now up the road. Under the half-moon the trees cast black shadows. An owl hooted nearby. "Who cooks for you, who cooks for you-oo?" The soft, savage flutter at the end of the hoot sent a shiver down Chad's neck. He was glad of Queenie's pale tail glowing ahead like a candle. Up and up the road; it seemed longer than in daylight, but finally he came out of the trees onto the open hilltop above the fields.

The house slept. Beyond the picket fence Helen's flowers made a white blur in the moonlight. A river of scent poured off them. It smelled like spiced vanilla, the way vanilla might smell in heaven.

Chad crossed the yard, feeling exposed and noisy, though his steps and Queenie's made only slight scritchings on the gravel. He was glad to slip inside the barn, black and silent and sweet with the scent of hay.

He switched on his flashlight, holding it low and pointing the beam toward the floor. Back, back. "Good, Queenie!" he whispered to the dim golden gleam on his left. "Sit!" The pig gave a long, low grunt. No sound came from the henhouse.

To the box stall. If Jeep had changed his mind, it would be empty. Tiger would be out with the rest of the stock.

But here he was, a dim motion in the flashlight beam, then a face over the door. His ears were forward. He blinked, friendly and sleepy.

"Hi, guy," Chad whispered. "Get you out of here." He set the flashlight on a hay bale and lifted the halter. He didn't handle horses much and couldn't tell at first which end was up. Was he supposed to unbuckle it or—no, it went over Tiger's ears and snapped at the throat. He reached with the halter, and the friendly nose shot toward the ceiling, knocking it out of his hands. It hit the opposite wall with a buckle-y crash.

Chad held his breath. No response from the house. He crossed the aisle and groped for the halter, approached the stall door again. Tiger drew back and swung his haunches around. His tail stung Chad's face.

Chad slid back the bolt, not making a sound, stepped inside the stall, and leaned over the door, hurting his armpit, to shoot the bolt home again. "Whoa, Tiger. Easy."

The snaky sound of his whispers didn't seem soothing even to him. The stall was full of large horse breaths, barely seen bulk. Had Tiger ever kicked anybody? Chad couldn't remember.

He touched Tiger's haunch, hot and flinching under his hand. "Easy." He tried voicing it, very low. But maybe that sounded like a growl. He slid his hand along Tiger's quivering barrel.

Tiger turned, knocking Chad on shin and shoulder. A smell of manure rose from the trampled floor. Shavings shooshed. Around they went. Around. Chad's fingers slipped off Tiger's slick side again and again.

Stop. Think.

What does a horse want? David would ask.

Grain. But Chad couldn't raid the grain bin. The lid had a creak you could hear in the kitchen. Helen timed breakfast by its sound.

So grain was out. What else?

Grass. Horses like grass. Horses like sugar. Horses . . .

This horse. Tiger, breathing tremulous breaths into a corner of the stall. This horse liked company. Horse company.

In his mind Chad saw small golden Tiger and big black Billy, scratching each other's shoulders with their lips and teeth. Neither had horse company at home. They rushed to greet each other, forehead to forehead, nostrils puffing, and then scratched.

"Easy," Chad murmured, getting the flat of his hand on Tiger's hip. The hot hide shivered away from him, but quickly he started scratching.

Tiger stood tensely for a moment. Then his frame seemed to relax. Chad scratched harder, and with a noisy sigh Tiger turned to present his shoulder, to swirl his bristly lip on Chad's upper arm.

Yes. Yes. They scratched each other.

Tiger's teeth opened, to nip Chad the way he'd nip Billy's shoulder. Harder, he meant. Like this.

Chad paused in his own scratching. Tiger hesitated, swung his muzzle away. Chad started again. Tiger's nose came back. He was gentler now, and if he got rough, Chad had only to lighten his own scratching. He kept it up for a while, giving Tiger a good long session before he slipped the halter on the half-seen head.

Time to go. He opened the door. But his hands and mind were busy with Tiger, and he forgot to be careful. The bolt shot back with a crack of metal on metal and—

"Bo-wo-wo-wo-wo-wo-wo! Bo-wo-wo-wo-wo-wo-wo-wo-wo-!"

It almost hurt, being that surprised. The night exploded into fragments. A rectangle of light flung out across the yard. Queenie trotted over it, hackles raised, toward the house and Ginger's barking. Tiger lunged out of the stall, dragging Chad. In the open aisle Chad braced, and the horse circled him, all angles and wild eyes.

The barn light came on, bleached and blinding. Shapes: a block, a stick . . .

"Jesus, Chad!"

Jeep. The gun.

"What the hell are you doing?"

"The hell are *you* doing?" Chad's voice came out breathy, half swallowed. The rifle pointed abruptly toward the floor. Jeep's knuckled hands eased the safety back on. In his pajamas. Top open. Gray hairs curling on his chest.

Out in the yard Queenie stood over Ginger, her neck stiff and bristling. Ginger bristled right back. More light. Helen's voice. "Jeep? Something in the chickens?" She was coming. "Queenie! What are you doing here? Jeep?"

Jeep blinked in the strong light. The bottom half of his face looked shrunken. No teeth.

A wild snarl went up. The dogs rolled past the barn door in a tight tangle. Tiger wheeled around Chad, knocking a shovel off the wall. It landed with a clatter. He half reared, dragged Chad through the open door past the dogs; Ginger's teeth were sunk in Queenie's ear, Queenie's teeth in the side of Ginger's ruff.

Tiger turned to face them and backed across the driveway. His steel-shod hooves plunged left, right, left. Chad moved with him till the horse stopped pulling, circled again, and he was the hub of the wheel. Facing Jeep . . .

Jeep moved toward the dogs. The gun barrel pointed down, near the whirl of blond and black fur, the intent and fragile skulls.

"Shoot them, why don't you?" The words ripped straight from the center of Chad's chest. "Go ahead and shoot them! You shoot everything else!"

A shining stream of water arced out of the night, splashing on the dogs. Queenie sprang back, sneezing. Like a thunderclap came Jeep's voice: *"Ginger!"*

Ginger crouched and slunk circling toward him. Queenie sat down to scratch tenderly at her bitten ear. The water shut off. Helen stood just inside the circle of light, the garden hose in her hand.

The yard went quiet but for the purring snorts of the horse, like falling gravel after an explosion.

Helen said, "Chad?"

Her voice was shocked. She stood there wrapped tightly in her pretty bathrobe, bringing the normal world into this scene.

Chad said, "He's going to sell him!" His voice sounded as if it had big air bubbles in it. "Jeep's going to sell him."

Helen let out a weary breath. "Don't you know your grandfather better than that? Do you really think—"

"He'd do anything! He shot Shep—"

A look came over Helen's face that stopped Chad cold: a look of danger, deeper and stronger than anything else in this yard. He could hear his heart pound.

"Put the horse back, Chad," she said. "He isn't going anywhere."

Chad stood staring for a minute, his mind gone completely blank. He became aware that he was trembling. The night throbbed with the sound of crickets.

Abruptly he turned Tiger's head and led him down the road, out of the circle of light.

"Chad!"

"Let him go." Jeep's voice sounded heavy. Chad looked back over his shoulder. Jeep stood rubbing his face with one hand. His shoulders slumped. His hair was ruffled, fluffy around his ears. Helen put her arm around him, gun and all, and Chad turned away.

24

It was three-thirty by the chiming clock before Chad could stop pacing the deck. He kept replaying the scenes: Tiger whirling in his stall, light, dogs, gun, "Go ahead and shoot them! You shoot everything else!" The raw rasp of his own voice, tearing his throat.

Then he'd walked away. No flashlight. It was in the barn, still shining, probably. He didn't need it. The feel and sound of the road under his feet, the path of stars above where the trees didn't quite meet, Queenie's tail ahead had guided him, and he'd turned Tiger loose in his own pasture and climbed the deck stairs, wanting to be someplace high and familiar.

Finally he sat in one of the lawn chairs and snapped his fingers for Queenie. Delicately he felt her ear, the velvet fur, the fine tendons. She winced and whined softly but let his fingers explore. A little stickiness was all he found—no terrible wound, as he had feared.

"Good Queen." He drew her close, rubbing her chest. She'd never fought before. "Good Queenie."

She lay down with a sigh, pressing hard against his legs. Maybe she felt the same way he did, sick with reabsorbed adrenaline. There'd been such a tang of it on the air up there. No wonder it had spilled over to the dogs.

The sky gradually turned from black to near black, to a sort of purplish, throbbing gray. Just after four-thirty a bird started singing. What kind was it? It said, "Tweet! Tweet!" like a cartoon bird.

Almost at once, as if they'd been waiting for a signal, other birds started up: thrushes, robins. A blue jay shrieked. Chad had been up all night now. His eyes prickled, and he closed them, leaning his head against the back of his chair.

Creak. Creak. Creak. Creak.

His eyes opened. The sky was already lighter, almost white. He could see tree branches and chairs. Inside, someone was coming downstairs.

The front door opened and closed. Chad got up and walked around the corner of the deck. Julia stood at the railing, fully dressed, staring down at Tiger.

She heard him and turned. Her face was a pale blur. "Chad? When did Jeep bring him? I was just going up there."

Chad shook his head. He hadn't imagined this scene or worked out what he would say. But she kept staring. He had to say something. "I went and got him."

"But . . . what did you say to Jeep?"

"Nothing. I just took him."

Julia's eyes widened. "Oh Lord. Now what?"

"Well, if you want me to take him back—"

"No, but—oh, Chad!" Julia sat down on the top stair. Queen went to her, and Chad stood behind them, forced now to think of the morning coming. Would Jeep show up or call? What would he say, and what would they say back? And—

"What happened to Queenie's ear?"

"Fight. Ginger."

"Oh, Chad." Julia looked devastated. "They never slept through that?"

Chad shook his head. He wasn't about to lay out the whole scene for her. "After breakfast we'll go see David," he said, and faked a yawn. "I'm going to bed."

But he couldn't sleep. The morning was long between dawn and breakfast, and at breakfast it was hard not to be impatient at Mom and Gib's ignorance. They knew nothing. Tiger had not been here last night and was here before break-fast, and they made nothing of it. They didn't even think about it. Chad almost felt sorry for them.

Mom did notice Queenie's ear, which had a dark three-cornered tear. She was puzzled. "She didn't have that when I went to bed! What could she have done?" Chad and Julia sat tight-lipped.

"Bring him," Chad said to Julia as they went down the deck stairs after breakfast. Jeep's truck hadn't passed yet. They couldn't leave Tiger unguarded.

They went down the road four abreast: Queenie, Chad, Julia, Tiger. The sound of hooves on gravel was like last night. Looking past Julia at the relaxed horse, Chad felt his heart swell unexpectedly, as if Tiger belonged to him.

"You have to tell me what happened," Julia said when they were out of sight of the house.

"No, I don't."

"Chad! I'm in the middle of this! I have to know!"

"Look, they came out, all right! Jeep had his gun, and Helen turned the hose on the dogs, and I came home."

"But they *let* you?"

"Could they stop me?" It came out with a little laugh. That was the thing about last night. Even Jeep's gun, even Helen's terrible warning face had not been able to hold him. How simple it had been to turn away with the horse, to step out of the circle of light into darkness! How strangely simple!

They walked down the road without speaking for a few minutes. Then Julia asked, "Why'd you do it?" She sounded hard and tough, as if she didn't care.

In a hard voice of his own Chad said, "I didn't want him to get away with it."

"But he was right. This horse—I can't handle him. I get *crazy*! Every day I come home from a ride and look in all my books and plan for tomorrow, and it never—and I'm *scared*!"

That turned Chad's head. Julia's mouth was open, corners turned down to hold back crying. Beyond her Tiger walked along mildly, his eye gentle.

"I never knew you were scared." He had to force it out.

Julia swallowed hard and lifted her chin, drew a deep breath. "I'm terrified," she said. "Every single minute. Like I'm strapped to a bomb."

"Then why—" Why what? It had been one of Chad's firmest beliefs that Julia was exactly what she appeared to be. That was what was wrong with her. She had no depths. After a moment he asked, "Do you *want* to keep him?"

Julia bit her lip. Tears spilled suddenly down her cheeks. She nodded.

Then they were in David's yard, and Chad could smell toast. "Hello!" he called, but no one came to the door, and he had to knock.

David appeared with a piece of toast in his hand. "Oh, hi—" He looked past Chad at Julia and Tiger, and though his face didn't change, his body slackened with dismay. They were a burden, he and Julia, awkward waifs, knuckled and bristling.

David let out a little sigh, even before he spoke. "Hello, Julia. Louise has told me about your problem. I'm not sure I can—"

"Daddy!" Louise was on the stairs behind him. Chad could see only her feet below the hem of the terry-cloth bathrobe. "Daddy, don't be a wimp!"

"Louise, my legal obligation—"

"Daddy!" Louise came all the way down. Her hair lay flat and feathery, shaped to her head. There was a crease on her cheek from the pillowcase. "Daddy, you do not have to train this horse, and you don't have to give Julia riding lessons. She's a terrific rider. You just have to teach her how to train—"

"Oh, Louise," David said. "I think my lawyer would tell me I need her parents' permission."

Louise looked stubborn but baffled, and Julia looked as if she wanted to sink into the ground.

Chad said, "Mom and Gib would give permission. Just ask them." He tried to telegraph to Julia, V style: "Don't mention Jeep!"

The message got garbled. Julia said, "Jeep owns him."

"And obviously he's fine with it," Louise said, "or he wouldn't have brought him back!"

Chad opened his mouth, and it hung open, empty of words. Julia was motionless beside him.

Louise looked, rubbed her hand across her eyes, and looked again. "Do you want me to call him, Daddy?" she asked in a quieter voice.

David closed his eyes. "Louise. There are times when I see your mother in you!" He went inside, making a little after-you-madame gesture to sweep her out onto the front step, and closed the door firmly. After a moment they heard his voice, too faraway for distinct words.

"I wish he wouldn't compare me to Mum!" Louise said.

Tiger pulled toward the lawn. It was mainly weed, not grass, and he gave up, stood with lowered head. His ears twitched, his lip drooped, as he succumbed to sleep. Julia leaned against his shoulder; Chad lowered himself onto the lawn; Louise stood on the doorstep, eyes wide and unfocused. A lot of time passed.

David's voice came nearer, as he wandered with his cordless phone. "Really?" He sounded as if he had all day and nothing on his mind.

"I see," he said. "I see. I see." Julia hugged Tiger's neck, looking sick.

Finally David said, "You were brought up using animals, so you always had to figure out how to make them understand. You probably don't even think about it anymore." He listened again. "Yeah? Yeah? I always figured oxen weren't the sharpest crayons in the box!"

It was going to be all right. Jeep was telling a story. Chad might even know which one. The young oxen on the farm in St. Johnsbury; the cows that went wild in the back pastures over in Warren and the boy sent after them; the bobcat that followed him; the bear and cubs . . . Chad knew all the stories, everything that made an adventure out of Jeep's hard growing-up.

David's voice faded again and in a minute stopped. He came outside with fresh toast. His coffee steamed white in the morning air. "Louise," he said, "why don't you go and . . . get yourself some breakfast?"

He meant, Go get some clothes on! Chad could hear that in his voice. Louise went inside, but came back, still in her bathrobe, with a mug of milky coffee and a granola bar. She sat on the step and patted the spot beside her. Chad sat, too. The stone was warm, and a shaft of sun came through the trees to tell of the hot day coming.

Out on the lawn David asked Julia questions. Is he head shy? Can you catch him? Does he kick? Bite? Rear?

"So," Louise said. Chad started. He'd been nearly asleep. "Tiger. What's the story?"

It all came flooding back again: the vanilla scent from the tobacco plants, the circle of yellow yard light with the dogs fighting and the horse snorting, and his grandparents. Jeep's gun. Helen's look.

And he had stepped out of the circle. Simply completed what he'd come to do.

He took a breath full of all this, and his voice came out of a deeper place in his chest. "I went up last night and took him."

He felt Louise turn to look at him and waited a second before looking back. Would she halfway disapprove, like Julia?

She was smiling, and her eyes sparkled, as if she found him funny and amazing. "Oh!" she said. "*Oh!* I don't think Daddy needs to know that!" She looked at him a moment longer and then stood up, pulling the robe tighter around her. "I'd better go get dressed."

Chad listened to her feet on the stairs. David sent Julia to the shed for grain. While she was gone, he did a little dance with Tiger, stepping toward him from the front and sides. Twice Tiger stepped away from David, and once he didn't. Chad couldn't tell which response David wanted. Everything was like that this morning. Only big movements, big patches of color registered. Everything else was distant, pleasantly distant.

David introduced Julia and Tiger to the clicker. Louise came back in khakis and a high-necked sleeveless shirt that bottled her up, made her older and taller.

"Grab that milk jug out of the trash and rinse it," David called. Louise brought the jug. Tiger backed away from it, showing the whites of his eyes, and within moments, it seemed, touched it, was clicked and treated, and with a few repeats nudged it vigorously, then swung his head around for his treat.

"Good! Jackpot!" David said, and walked toward the step, beckoning with one finger for Julia to follow.

He sat beside Louise, squashing her over tight against Chad. Thank you, David!

"Lecture," he said, and looked around at all of them. "Some bad stuff has been going on with this horse, I gather— no, no!" He held up his hand to silence Julia. She subsided miserably. "Look at him!"

Tiger stood with his head low. His eyes were wide and thoughtful. "He's fine," David said. "He's going to be fine."

"But I've—"

"You've been rough with him." David sounded exceptionally gentle. "You were like a drowning person. They're very dangerous, people who are drowning."

Julia bowed her head. Tears ran down her cheeks.

David said, "He likes and trusts you, by and large, because

by and large you bring good things. Some things make you crazy, that's all. He jigs on the way home; you can't stop him, and you feel helpless. He only knows that going home gets you upset. That makes him nervous, so he jigs—see? Like a dog chasing its tail."

Julia gulped back a sob. "But I've ruined him, haven't I? Horses remember the bad things forever!"

"Nonsense! A horse is just as relieved as anyone else to have a misunderstanding cleared up."

"Really?"

"A horse remembers a blow when the blow stays latent in the handler. But you're going to change, and he'll be the first to notice."

"I've tried—"

"This is not about trying," David said. "This is not about whether or not you're a good person. It's about know-how. When things go wrong, you're going to stop and think because thinking's going to work for you. You'll have a tool-box full of options that will let you do anything with this horse—as long as you're willing to start here, where you are."

For a guy who doesn't believe in words . . . Chad meant to say it aloud, but perhaps he didn't. Moments later Louise's whisper seared into his head. "Chad! Wake up!"

Chad jerked upright, eyes flying open. Jeep's pickup had just passed the driveway. The brake lights glowed a moment but blinked out almost immediately.

CHAPTER

25

CHAD WALKED UP the hill, going slower and slower. The air felt thick, like syrup. It forced down his eyelids. He dragged himself up the deck stairs, up the inside stairs, and collapsed diagonally across his bed.

When he awoke, the light was different, and he felt ravenous. He went downstairs to make a sandwich. There on the table was the flashlight he'd left in Jeep's barn. In the cellar, where they packed lightbulbs for shipping, he heard his parents' agitated voices.

He walked with his sandwich to the sliding glass door and looked out. Above the level of Queenie's nose and Sky's hands the glass was clean. He could see the garden, the heap of rocks beneath which the coon was buried, and, not far from it, Shep's grave. Shot and buried, while Chad tried to paint a clump of sumacs. He would never see Shep again, and he'd never had a last look. He'd never be able to paint or draw or pat Shep or say his name and meet the dog's warm eyes.

Usually his heart hurt when he thought that. Right now it was just true. His breath made a cloud on the glass door. He pulled it open and, as he stepped out, heard a familiar sound from below, at the barn. *Click!*

Julia had brought home the milk jug. Tiger nudged it eagerly, swung his head. Julia fed him something and explained to Jeep, "He's learning to target on this, and then I can teach him to target longer and longer, so he'll stand tied."

Tiger nudged the jug. Jeep said, "Figured out which button to push, hasn't he?" Chad couldn't see Jeep's face, but he heard the smile. Jeep's hand cupped Queenie's head, his fingers massaged the root of her ear. Ginger, in the driver's seat of Jeep's truck, looked intently out the window. To his surprise Chad knew exactly how she felt: jealous.

He opened his mouth to call Queenie and couldn't force his voice out, didn't want to announce his presence. Jeep put a hand on Julia's shoulder, that quick, hard squeeze that almost hurt. Chad remembered it, the without-words way Jeep reconnected.

Jeep turned toward his truck now. Chad made himself stay where he was. Jeep's glasses glinted as he looked up and away. No hesitation, no pause to consider, as there had been for months. Chad understood. Jeep had given up on him. "Let him go," Jeep had said last night, his words blurred by no teeth, and Helen had put her arm around him.

When he was small enough that it was a big deal to stay overnight at the farm, one of the great treats had been seeing Jeep take his teeth out at night, put them in a glass of water beside the bed. Chad remembered the clear water, the grinning teeth, so different from Jeep's real smile. Tiny bubbles rose from the dentures, and he used to lie beside Jeep and Helen in the early mornings, gazing at them.

He had learned a lot about Jeep since those days. Out of the hard upbringing had grown a hard man, one who could shoot the creatures he loved. Jeep loved every pig and every steer, and he'd loved Shep, and still he could get his gun off the window rack and . . .

That was too hard to think about. That brought back the iron grip of pain. Chad breathed into it, as the truck started below, as a dog came upstairs and around the corner.

Queenie. Not Shep. Not ever—

"You know what?" he said to himself. Queenie's big ears pricked, and her eyes met his. "You're *trying* to make yourself feel bad! How sick is that?" He bent to welcome the dog he did have.

It was hard to know where to be right now. His job was on hold while David worked with Julia, who had the urgent near-term goal of not dying in the show ring at the county fair next Saturday.

The fair was almost the end of August. One week later Louise would go.

Chad waited, mornings, to see if she would come play with Sky. Twice she did, and he stayed home, too, worked on Sky's door, and listened to the ambush game. Then he'd walk down the hill with her or show her another trail. The days she stayed home Chad went down to the white house to join her in watching Julia and Tiger. He made guesses about what was going on. Louise would only answer "hotter" or "colder," but at home Julia explained it all fully.

"His ear thing," she told Mom. "I was always trying to *hold* his ear, so of course he wouldn't let me! David says just touch it for a second, just brush it, so it's no big deal. I mean, I'm touching his ear for a second, but I'm not going to *keep* it, so he lets me."

"David said, 'Ride where you can, not where you can't,'" she told Jeep. "It's what John Lyons, the horse trainer, says. So I'm riding here in the pasture right now, and it's such a *relief*!"

"The click stops the behavior," she explained to Gib. "It's so great. I click him for a nice slow canter, and he'll automatically stop to get his treat!"

"But you want him to *keep* cantering," Gib said. "Right?"

"Eventually, but I don't have to get there all at once."

"All along," she said to Chess on the telephone, "I've been watching for things he's doing wrong. Now I look for what he's doing right. It's *so* incredible!"

Chad had been learning these concepts half the summer and had never brought a word of it home. Julia'd been at it less than a week.

But that was what Julia did: amplify things. Not even tie-dye was enough for her. She had to add polka dots and purple fringe. "What a pain!" Chad said to himself, crouching to paint cobblestones on Sky's door. He more or less expected this attitude from himself. But when Louise didn't come up Friday morning, he was glad to go down again and see what they were doing.

It involved riding circles in the pasture. That seemed to be what riders did with horses: go in circles. Tiger was supposed to carry his head lower, a posture that automatically calmed him.

After a while Louise got on Rocky bareback; Chad was allowed to make a stirrup with his hands so she could mount. He took her whole weight for a moment, and her leg brushed his cheek. Then she rode Rocky up behind Tiger at various paces, and Tiger got clicked if he stayed calm.

Jeep should be here. Chad couldn't help thinking that. Jeep would be fascinated, and relieved to see Julia making progress. But he wouldn't come. He was never in the same place Chad was, these days. Only now could Chad see how continually Jeep had tried, one way and another, to mend the breach between them.

No more. Let him go, Jeep had said, and he was doing that.

"I think you'll live!" David said at the end of the session. "If we had another week, you might even win a ribbon!"

"Living is enough!" Julia said, her face tightening as she thought about tomorrow.

What about *after* the fair? Chad wondered, startled. Would David want to go on working with Julia? He probably ought to, but what about Chad's job? What about Queenie? Chad was progressing on his own, teaching her to follow her target stick to the left, to the right, or in a complete circle around him, but what *for*? He wanted to do something with her, the way he wanted to paint when he saw something beautiful. She was too good not to do something with. But what? He couldn't see either of them at an obedience trial; he had no livestock for her to herd; he couldn't make her into a rescue dog or a drug sniffer.

Too early to worry, he decided, taking this moment while the others talked to scratch Tiger's neck. He'd get Julia through the fair, live through Louise's departure, and then see where that left them all.

He and Julia walked home, not talking. Jeep passed, going downhill, and nodded. The darkened glasses made it impossible to tell if Chad was included in the greeting, or only Julia. Sky waved from the seat beside Jeep; going out to lunch again.

That had been awfully convenient, Chad realized suddenly. Almost too convenient. Had Mom asked? Or did Jeep just know how much Chad had needed Sky out of the house?

Would Jeep do that?

The moment he knew to ask the question, Chad knew the answer. Jeep would do anything, for any of them. It was an unspoken constant of their lives. They could count on Jeep. Who had bought a horse for Julia after all? And when Sky was born, and Mom was exhausted and Gib worried and Julia Julia, and there was no space for Chad anywhere in the family, it was Jeep who had rescued him, had him up at the farm every single day working on something, as if his help were essential.

And that meant . . . didn't that mean—

"Listen," he said to Julia. "Listen. What happened?" She looked at him in confusion. "When Shep . . ."

Julia's face went yellow as the blood drained from under her tan. She stopped walking. "We've *told* you what happened," she said in a thin voice. "We've told you a hundred times."

"But . . . was Jeep . . . right? Did he do the right thing?"

Julia closed her eyes. "God. Yes. He did the right thing."

"But was Shep—"

Julia shook her head, the tiniest shake, barely visible. "Don't ask, Chad. Don't. He was . . . alive, and he shouldn't have been. I don't know if he really . . . he was faraway already, but he was breathing, and—" Julia swallowed. "It was horrible. One minute he was there, the way he always was, and then . . . He looked the wrong way. He was so smart, but just that one time he looked the wrong way."

For a moment Chad could see it: the dark red tailless dog standing in the road, head turned, robust and intelligent and full of life. He could hear a car coming, and he couldn't see what happened next.

Julia said. "Jeep cried. After he did it. He sat on the truck bumper . . . And the man cried. The driver. But Jeep . . . and then he put Shep in the truck. 'I don't want Chad to see this,' he said."

Chad looked around for something to sit on. The stone wall was too faraway. He collapsed at the edge of the ditch, and Queenie came up, wagging slightly. He wrapped his arms around her. "God. God . . . Jeep *cried?*"

"I'm so sorry, Chad. Shep caught up with me, and . . . it was always all right before. I'm sorry . . ."

"He could open the door," Chad said. His voice sounded dull to him. "I should have taken him with me. But he drank the paint water. Remember when he came home with a blue tongue?"

Julia gave a hiccup of laughter. Chad hugged Queenie tighter, into the wound in his heart. He bowed his head on top of hers. After a moment he heard Tiger's hooves crunch and felt Julia's hand awkward on his back.

He could look up and blink, say something light, and put this all back in its box. Or he could be like Jeep. Just cry. "God," he said, and then he didn't have a choice anymore.

CHAPTER

26

_____

THEY ARRIVED EARLY at the fairgrounds. Jeep's truck rumbled softly over the grass near the horse show ring. Gib parked the van beside it. Chad got out into the cool morning air, feeling that familiar tingle of fair day excitement.

In a roped-off ring near the parking lot some people were setting up bright plastic tunnels and a seesaw. "What's this?" Mom asked, heading that way.

"No!" Sky yelled. "Beans!"

He had a yogurt container full of green beans he'd planted. Gib had gotten him to weed them maybe twice all summer, but now that fair day had arrived Sky was very attached to them. Mom had been reading him *Farmer Boy*, and Sky was sure his beans, like Almanzo's pumpkin, would win a large cash prize.

"Let's get the beans settled in," Mom said.

Chad went with them, as a way of not staying here with white-faced Julia, and Gib, and Jeep. They climbed the dirt road to the upper plateau, to the cattle barn, the rides, and the food booths. Mom poked her head into the kitchen to say hi to Helen, who'd been working there since dawn. Sky grabbed her hand and pulled her toward the Exhibit Hall.

The long tables were bright with jellies, peaches in glass jars, cookies and cakes and quilts and flowers and paintings. Sky found the vegetable section and arranged his beans on a glossy red plate. A nice color for green beans. If only they hadn't been so large and tough-looking, so bruised by affectionate handling.

Almanzo Wilder had seen the ribbon pinned on his pumpkin. Sky wanted nothing less. He watched his beans proudly, pointing whenever a grown-up approached.

"It may be a long time before the judges come," Mom said. The Exhibit Hall was her least favorite part of the fair; now it looked as if she might be here all morning.

At last merry-go-round music started. Chad said, "Want a ride, Sky? I'll go on with you."

"Thank you," Mom breathed.

They were the only riders. Around them the empty horses cycled up and down, and the fairground spun. Sky grinned tightly, gripping the handles that stuck out of his horse's neck. He looked small. Chad wanted to stand beside him, make sure he didn't fall off the slippery wooden saddle. But Sky would yell.

The ride finished. Mom pointed to a little boy near the cattle barn: Sky's loudest, wildest friend. "Isn't that Boone?" When Sky darted away, she jerked a thumb at Chad. "You've been a saint. Now beat it."

The food vendors were starting their stoves. Smells of garlic and frying filled the air, strange and not quite tempting this early in the morning. Chad passed the booth where you paid to shoot at tin ducks and win things no one in his right mind would want. A tinny sound system crooned the fifties song "Teen Angel." He found the booth where the old couple sold fried dough. With a hot sugared plateful he went over to the cattle show.

This was the slow, clean part of the fair. In the open-sided barn cows stood on bright sawdust. Their white markings sparkled. Even their tails were combed.

In the ring kids led calves around. Once Chad had shown a calf of Jeep's. He could feel in his bones the way the calves resisted, leaning back on the halters at every step.

Suddenly, with a little skip of heart, he noticed Jeep across the ring. Had Jeep seen him? He was talking to someone, teeth gleaming, hardly seeming to notice what was in the ring, let alone on the other side of it.

But as a Guernsey calf bogged down in front of him, Jeep reached over the rope and pressed her in the ribs with one finger. For a few steps the calf hurried; the little girl leaning on the halter rope nearly fell down. A moment later, still talking, Jeep prodded another calf.

So Jeep might have seen him, too. He saw more than he appeared to. Chad walked a quarter turn around the cattle ring, out of Jeep's line of sight. There he watched and tried to pick the winner, without knowing at all what made a good cow. When the ribbons were given and the ring emptied, Jeep was opposite him again.

Chad slipped away, to the edge of the plateau. Below him in

one ring, massive work teams hauled a sled full of stones. In another tiny riders tried to steer disobedient ponies. Way over to the left a loose dog ran through one of the blue tunnels.

Should have brought Queenie, he thought.

A throng of little people, two brushstrokes each, streamed in the fairground gates. Chad saw two of his classmates and three people he'd played baseball with, the deputy fire chief, his third-grade teacher. But where—

There! Two pairs of long, slender legs and sandals, David reaching into the pocket of his shorts, Louise looking around as if searching for someone. Inside the fence David studied an orange map, then headed toward the horse show ring as the announcer said, "The next class is English Pleasure."

A motion to the left caught Chad's eye: Jeep again, hurrying down the crowded dirt road toward the show ring. Chad watched him take a place along the fence. Off in another corner was Gib, a bright splash of tie-dye.

The ring filled with horses. Not good! Last year Tiger had run away with Julia, galloping around this ring like a car in the Indy 500. The fewer horses in with him, the better.

Julia rode in last, her face pale between dark hat and dark coat. She passed David and Louise, wedged in near the rail, and smiled for a second, smiled again at Gib and at Jeep. Chad slithered down the steep slope to a place at the fence, to provide another spot of encouragement.

"Trot, please, trot!"

Ears flattened. Tails swished. The ring got loud with hoofbeats. Chad lost Julia, found her again. She was keeping out of the dangerous clumps of too many horses, too close together. Tiger trotted calmly.

"Walk, please, walk."

Next would come the canter. Julia's face was white when she passed. Her eyes looked inward, as if she were listening to something only she could hear. Chad saw a flash of yellow in her right hand.

"And canter, please, canter."

With deep grunts and sometimes a little explosion out the back end, most horses complied. Some pounded along at a furious trot while the riders kicked futilely. One bucked, throwing the rider forward onto the pommel of the saddle.

Chad kept his eyes on Tiger, who swished his tail and lifted into a canter down the long side of the ring.

After a few strides, though, he lurched down to a trot. Julia steered him toward the fence as other horses passed. She reached into her jacket pocket and then forward, and Tiger reached back to her hand, coming to a full stop.

Now forward again, walking. As they reached the corner Tiger began to canter, rounded, relaxed, not too fast.

A horse galloped past them, faster than the rest. Chad could almost see its speed swooshing Tiger along.

No. He was stopping again. A treat. They walked toward Chad, then lifted lightly into a canter as the announcer said, "And walk, walk."

Horses tossed their heads, slammed on the brakes, ran right through the brakes, and Tiger kept gently cantering. As they neared Chad's spot, he heard it: *click!* Tiger stopped, ears swiveling gladly, and received some small treat from Julia's palm. Her face was flushed now, and her eyes looked as if she'd seen an angel.

"And reverse, please, reverse."

The whole thing repeated, while Chad worked his way

around the outside of the ring, past Gib, behind Jeep's stone-like back. He'd almost reached David and Louise when cantering broke out again and he had to stop and watch.

It was all right. Once Tiger pinned his ears and shook his head angrily, but Julia clicked him, anyway, and that changed his mood.

"And line up, please, line up."

Julia would not win a ribbon, but no one in the ring looked happier. Chad went on. As he caught the scent of Louise's violet perfume, a large lady at the fence said in a disgusted voice, "A show is *no* place to train a horse!"

Louise's hand went up as if to stop the woman from speaking. Then she pressed her fingers to her mouth as David turned.

"I beg to differ," he said. "A show is the *only* place to teach show ring manners!"

Louise put her hand up to shield her eyes and turned away, almost bumping into Chad. "Oh! Hi!" She pointed at David's back and shook her head. "I can't take him anywhere!"

They headed toward Julia, but Jeep got there first, with a white glint of smile, a clap on the neck for Tiger. Julia's dark-coated body, so upright in the ring, slumped toward Jeep. She reached down and put a hand on his shoulder. Then she wrapped her arms around Tiger's neck in a big hug.

Hooves sounded behind Chad and Louise. Pia trotted past, a yellow ribbon fluttering on her horse's bridle. *"Jules!"* Heads turned for fifty yards around. "What was goin' on out there?"

Julia's face glowed. "Clicker training. You use positive reinforcement to tell the horse what it's doing right—"

This was going to be a lecture, a good old-fashioned, annoying Julia lecture. "C'mon," Chad said to Louise. "I'll show you the fair."

C H A P T E R

27

THEY STARTED WITH the Exhibit Hall. Sky's beans had won two ribbons, a white fourth place for beanness and a blue with a card reading, "Youngest Exhibitor." They watched the cattle show and toured the small animal exhibit. They assembled an early lunch of Thai chicken barbecue, falafel, onion rings, and fried dough. Louise shot a tin rabbit and won a teddy bear and gave it to a passing child. They moved on to the Horse Pull.

This was the hard-bitten part of the fair, and when he was younger, Chad had been allowed here only with Jeep. There was bad language, beer in the coolers, and sometimes a fight broke out. Jeep always made Chad feel safe, though. He knew this tough crowd. Some were even family of sorts, relatives of people Jeep lived with as a child. On the hillside in lawn chairs and down near the ring, Chad saw familiar faces. Jeep would have said hello. Talk would follow, and stories. By himself

Chad felt half dumb, half a stranger. He couldn't show Louise what Jeep could have. But she'd never seen any of it, and he could show her plenty.

Eight huge teams of horses stood tied to the chain-link fence. A yellow tractor dragged the stoneboat back up the lane of sand to the starting point and rumbled out of the way. The announcer said, "Next up, Bob Ring from Rockingham. Thirty-eight hundred pounds on the boat."

Three men went to the back of a big blond team. Two picked up the whippletrees, the ironbound lengths of wood that would connect horses and harness to the load. The whippletrees were heavy; the men's free arms hung out to the sides for balance. The driver leaned back two-fisted on the reins. Men and horses moved in a stiff unit, the men's strides dragged long by the horses' slow, ground-covering jounce.

They reached the stoneboat, turned. A clamor of voices rose harshly: "Whoa!"; "Back!"; "C'mon, back!" The team lunged once before it was hitched. More yells and suddenly: "Hut!" The horses surged forward, digging in their toes, while the driver slapped one set of haunches with the reins and yelled, "*Pull*, Dick! *Pull!*"

They crossed the finish line, and the horses slacked off instantly. The men unhitched, and the horses jounced back to the fence, snorting and purring out their breaths. The driver tied them to the fence and went behind them to pick up his conversation.

"Not even a pat?" Louise asked. That didn't seem strange to Chad. The horses were like a tractor, and that was how the men stood behind them; no question of a kick.

"C'mon, let's go closer." They wandered along the chain link in front of the teams. The little eyes, closed between the black curve of blinders and the blur of the fence, looked at them incuriously. These horses didn't expect much from people. One mouthed its teammate's rein, then ducked and rubbed its head against the other horse's neck. Another bit at the fence till a teamster yelled, "Hey!"

"Look at their noses," Louise said. "They must wear halters every minute that they aren't wearing bridles."

Chad had never noticed that before, the pink band of chafed skin across many of the horses' faces. At each bite of grass, each mouthful of hay, the noseband of the halter rubbed, a hundred, a thousand, a million times. No one noticed.

These people used themselves the same way, though. Their own bodies were blunt instruments, treated no better than the horses, and no worse. Chad wondered if Louise saw that. He didn't think he could explain. If she could walk around here with Jeep, she'd see.

And there Jeep was, talking to a thin old man with a greased helmet of yellow-white hair and three visible teeth. "Come on over," Chad almost said. Jeep would welcome Louise at least. But he couldn't make himself do it.

"All right," Louise said finally. "What else?"

"Horse show?"

"We've seen the horse show. Come on, now I'll show you something!" She led him toward the ring with the tunnels. Chad had never seen that at the fair before, but apparently it was something Louise knew all about.

The crowd was thick here. They stood behind short people and watched a dog scramble over a tall plywood A-frame and leap out of the ring through a tire. A man ran to catch the dog, a woman in the ring stood holding both hands above her head, and everybody clapped.

"Next up is Sasha, owned by Ann Mott," a woman announced over a loudspeaker.

Before Chad could figure out what had just happened, or even locate the new competitor, a black-and-white streak shot through the tire. A woman in T-shirt and shorts ran parallel to the dog, toward two sets of jump poles. "Jump!" she shouted. The dog soared over the first pole. "Jump!" Over the second.

"Tunnel!" She pointed toward an orange curved tunnel nestled at the bottom of some of the strange jungle gym equipment. The dog disappeared into one end and came out the other almost instantly, as if the tunnel were a time warp.

"Don't blink!" said the announcer, and the handler said, "Jump!"

Another jump, a yellow tunnel. That shot Sasha straight toward a narrow catwalk with ramps at each end. She raced up the ramp, slowed to a trot across the walkway, began to race again down the slope.

"Touch!" The woman held up a warning hand.

Sasha slowed to a creep, eyes glued to the woman's hand.

"Remember," the announcer said to the audience, "the dog needs to touch the yellow with at least one paw." The bottom third of the ramp, of all the ramps, was painted yellow.

Sasha's handler made her pause on the yellow for several seconds. Then she dropped her hand. "Jump!"

Sasha exploded off the ramp, over another jump.

"Seesaw!"

The dog trotted up one end of the seesaw, paused in the center while the other end slowly sank to the ground, then trotted down, touched the yellow end.

"Weave!"

A set of twelve poles stood near the edge of the ring. Sasha wove between them, not missing one, while the handler made a "*ch-ch-ch-ch-ch*" sound. Then: "Jump! Chute!"

Sasha soared over the jump and disappeared into a blue tunnel with a long sock of fabric on the far end. In a second a blue form fought through the fabric; everyone laughed as the running dog shape animated the cloth.

Another jump, through the orange tunnel, the A-frame, and out through the tire.

The woman staggered across the finish line. "*Yes*, Sasha! Yes!" Hugs, leaps, a treat, leash on, and the next competitor came up to the line.

"Wow!" Chad said. *"Wow!"*

Louise was smiling. "The dog was good!"

"But what *is* this?"

"Next up is Spike," the announcer said. "Spike is a Humane Society dog, half Australian shepherd and half beagle. If anyone's wondering what you're watching, this is a Dog Agility match, and this is our first year holding it at the fair. If you're interested in learning, I teach a class right here at the fairground on Thursday evenings. Just show up with your dog!"

Spike was young and flexible and soared over every jump with his head swiveled halfway around to watch his handler. He was followed by a springer spaniel, a whippet on long, delicate steel-spring legs, a Lab, wagging all the way, and a Border collie, who barked once for every single pole of the weave, a dozen barks in just a few seconds.

The owners came in all shapes, too. Some seemed to court cardiac arrest. Others were fit. One guy in particular seemed a little too fit, a bit overtanned. After his run he led his dog around the outside of the ring and stood by Louise. Chad turned his head to check the guy out. He was surprised for a second that the rest of the fair was still here. He hadn't looked away from the ring in what felt like an hour.

"This next dog's quite good," said Mr. Tan to Louise, in what sounded like a fake English accent.

Louise glanced his way. "Your dog is good, too."

"Well, Spam's been at it quite a while."

And you've been picking up girls quite a while! Chad thought. The guy had lines around his eyes, actual wrinkles!

"Have you seen Agility be—"

"Shh," Louise said, watching the next dog. Chad watched, too. Even with a guy putting the moves on Louise, he couldn't help being drawn. The joy, the motion—and this handler used a clicker and treats to slow the dog on the ramp and seesaw. "This is a training match," the announcer reminded everyone.

The dog soared out through the tire. Louise said, "Yes, I've seen Agility before. My father is David Burton, the trainer. Maybe you've heard of him?"

"Oh yes!" Tan said. He sounded startled. "How old are you—if you don't mind my asking?"

"Nearly sixteen."

Tan's gulp was audible. "Oh." He fell silent for a moment. "Well! Nice meeting you!" He and Spam wandered on their way.

Louise turned and smiled at Chad. "I handled that well, didn't I?"

"Oh, ace!" For no reason except that he'd always wanted to, Chad touched her hair. It felt the way it looked, like meringue, crisp and brittle with spray. He wanted to crush one of the peaks in his fingers, feel the silky hair inside. But he only brushed it lightly, for just a second.

Louise gave him a startled look. "What are you doing?"

Chad smiled and shrugged and stepped back slightly, giving her space if she wanted it. She moved away, but only a little.

There was a pause in the action while jumps were lowered. A dense buzz of talk arose. Some people moved away, but most just shifted and stretched.

Chad discovered Phil standing nearby. Phil looked from him to Louise with an impressed face and a quick thumbs-up. Then he zipped his lips and melted into the crowd.

Hotfaced, Chad looked away toward the fairground. He could see Julia at a distance, riding around bareback with Pia.

And Jeep. Every time he'd looked around today, Jeep was somewhere in the picture. Now he was walking up the road toward the cattle show, alone. Chad's hand flew up to wave. He snatched it back but not quite soon enough.

Jeep hesitated. It seemed forever, but it was just a second there in the middle of the fairground road. Then he came toward Chad, his face showing nothing. As he arrived, the next dog started.

Chad sneaked a look at Jeep's profile. A man like Jeep, who'd worked animals all his life, could think this was foolishness. It wouldn't be surprising.

But almost at once Jeep's smile started to spread. It looked to Chad as if he were trying to hold it back. But come the seesaw, come the poles and the long blue sock, and Jeep's whole face was smiling.

He watched another dog, a beautiful young Rhodesian ridgeback, and chuckled when she paused atop the A-frame and regally surveyed the crowd.

He glanced at his watch then and took a step away. Don't! Chad thought.

"This one looks like Ginger," he said. Jeep glanced at him, surprised. "Don't you think?"

It was a stretch. The dog was small; that was all the resemblance. She went around the course like a silken streak, and Jeep settled back on his heels, arms folded.

The dog whipped through the weave poles. A child's voice shrilled, "Do*ggie!*" When she completed her run and the ring was empty for a moment, the child cried, "Do it again!"

"Did I mention that you and your dog can take classes?" the announcer wondered jokingly. This was the fifth mention; it kept coming around, like the chorus of a song. "I teach right here at the fairgrounds every Thursday evening—"

Chad didn't look at Jeep. He looked straight ahead and spoke in a carefully flat voice. "Want to try it? Bring Queenie and Ginger?"

A fat beagle came out. They stood shoulder to shoulder, watching her. Chad felt the heat off Jeep's arm. He heard the slow breath Jeep took in through his nose.

"Baseball on Thursdays. For a couple more weeks." Jeep sounded careful, too, like a man dickering over the price of something. He waited a moment and said, "Ted Bushway broke his leg. Couldn't hit, anyway."

"I could fill in," Chad said, watching the beagle. "And then we could do this."

"All right."

They didn't look at each other. They kept their eyes on the beagle. Obligingly, she soared off the back side of the A-frame, short legs all spraddled, and that let Chad laugh out loud.

———————

Thursday evening Chad rode with Jeep to baseball practice. They didn't talk on the way down. Chad didn't know
what to say, and he figured it was the same with Jeep.

Eventually they would talk. Eventually, one way or another,
Jeep would show himself, and say the things he knew about
life and death, bright and dark, here and gone. Not yet, but it
would happen. For now they were together in the truck.

Jeep pulled into the parking lot. Chad got out, and his door
slammed a moment after Jeep's did. Phil's and Gordie's heads
swiveled toward the sound. Gordie's elbow nudged Phil's
ribs, and the two of them waited. The pulse pounded in
Chad's throat as he crossed the parking lot toward them. It
seemed like a long walk.

He opened his mouth, wondering what he was going to say,
but Gordie spoke first. "Chad. How's it goin'?"

It was a real question. Gordie really wanted to know. All this time, Chad thought. The backs of his eyes stung. He stretched them wide open. "Better. It's going better."

He passed between them, clapping his hands on their backs. Somebody cuffed his hat down over his eyes, and Phil said, "Then let's play ball!"

Chad was amazed at the new power in his swing. He was better than before: bigger, stronger, faster. His arms bulged the sleeves of last year's shirt. Later, riding back in the dusk with Jeep, he felt the mysteriousness of growth, of all processes that go on without your participation or consent.

On Saturday Louise and David came to watch the game. It was Louise's last week and impossible to pry her and her father apart. She was going away. Sooner and sooner she would be leaving, and did either one of them care about baseball? It didn't seem likely, but there they were in lawn chairs among the other spectators.

The game went into extra innings, and Chad hit the grounder that drove in the winning run. Minutes later dusk closed in. Everyone clustered around the coolers, recapping, crowing, and a lot of people hit Chad on the back. "Holloway! Varsity next year!" the high-school coach said. Chad didn't want to stand there grinning and congratulating himself, but he couldn't hold back the smile from the corners of his mouth.

He grabbed a soda and looked around. David was right there with the rest of them, talking with Barrett's most fanatical baseball mom. Louise stood a little way off, watching him. Chad made a long arm through the crowd for another soda and strolled over to her. As he reached her, he was aware of the smell of sweat on him, but that was August and baseball.

"Got you a soda."

"Thanks." She cracked it open without glancing at the can and drank. "What *is* this? Did you ever notice how you can't tell what kind of soda you're drinking if you can't see the label?"

"They're all the same. They just use different coloring."

Someone turned on the field lights. Bugs gathered, and moments later the bats started swooping through, snapping them up.

"Do you want to go for a walk?" Louise asked.

Chad almost said, Doesn't David want to go home? Some saving mercy prevented him from being that stupid. "Yes," he said, and they turned up the sidewalk toward town.

The sidewalk was narrow. Their shoulders brushed again and again. Tonight she wore sandals, and she didn't seem that much taller.

"There isn't room," she said, and threaded her arm under his, around his waist. There was nowhere for his arm to go but around her. He drew a breath that seemed to come in forever, and they both laughed. They pressed against each other as if their bodies wanted the same thing at the same time and went a little zigzag up the sidewalk.

"I stink," Chad said.

"You do. You certainly do." Louise pressed her face against his shoulder and made a choking sound. "*Phew!* So this is how a baseball hero smells?"

"If I hadn't batted in that run, would we be doing this?"

"What are we doing?"

"I don't know!" Chad said. "I'm just a hometown boy!"

She stopped laughing. In a minute she said, "Tomorrow at this time I'll be in New York."

Chad stopped feeling like laughing, too. "When does school start?"

"Next week."

"Guys in leotards," Chad said. His mouth was just saying things. It was sort of interesting to watch what kept coming out of him. "Guys with muscles where I don't even have places—"

"A lot of them are gay, Chad."

"Yeah? Well, a lot of them aren't."

She gave his waist a little squeeze. Chad couldn't believe how good that felt. She was silent for a minute. "Look, I'm not—I can't— Look! You're a whole year younger than me!"

It mattered. Chad knew it mattered. Even though it was silly, it made a difference. But . . .

"When you're twenty-five," he said, "I'll be twenty-four."

She gave a startled little laugh, because that was ridiculous, the difference between twenty-five and twenty-four. He felt her body go still against his.

Then she leaned into him, really hugging him. "We'll know each other then. We will know each other."

They swung around to turn back, as if they each wanted to. No telling who decided. "We will," Chad said, after a while. It was too long a pause; he'd been hearing her words again: "We'll know each other then. We will know each other." And we'll know each other in between, if I have anything to do with it!

He knew better than to say that. Shaping didn't work on people if you announced your intentions.

As they reached the edge of the ballfield's light, she slipped out of his arm and stepped away. A second later she was laughing again. "Now *I* stink! What am I going to tell Daddy?"

The next morning from his lookout Chad watched her leave. The mother, a thin figure in black, waited behind the open driver's door of a white car, while Louise and David clung to each other in a hard hug. Then quickly Louise turned away, got in the car, and it vanished down the green tunnel of trees. She never looked uphill, though he'd shown her the place, and she could have guessed he was there.

The car was expensive and nearly silent and faded quickly from earshot, leaving an emptiness on the air that was almost shocking. Chad felt his fingers, far down at the end of his arm, smoothing and smoothing and smoothing the top of Queenie's head. His throat ached.

Had he made too much of yesterday? It had kept him awake half the night, but maybe it hadn't meant anything. Louise was older. Last night the difference in their ages had been almost nothing, but this morning it was back, big as ever, and in a week, a New York week, it might be colossal. Nothing had been said about keeping in touch.

David turned on the doorstep, bumped into the lintel, and put his hand out to steady himself. He looked hollow, like an empty peapod. Chad felt heat rise in his face. He turned away.

But at the first step something stopped him. "We have to go to her," Louise had said when Julia was crying in the field. Chad had felt then as he did now. But Louise had been right.

He took a deep breath, hoping that would help somehow, hoping he was up to this. "Queenie, let's go."

When David opened the door, he looked blank, as if he hadn't known anyone in the world was left alive. "Chad."

"Hi." After Chad said that, there was nothing left to say. He probably looked as bad as David did.

"Come in," David said, and they followed Queenie to the

kitchen. She tested the air. To Chad, it was full of Louise, a sort of aching absence, the barest whiff of violets. The kitchen felt emptier even than that first day when they'd brought the stove in. It wasn't bare now; it was missing something.

David stood pinching the bridge of his nose. Was he trying not to cry? If Chad weren't here, he *could* cry. This was wrong. "Sorry. I'll go—"

But from the yard came the sound of a truck engine. Chad looked out the window. Jeep let himself down from the cab and walked around to the back. He opened the tailgate and rolled out the red goat cart.

It was dusty still, spattered with bird poop and shedding a few feathers. Jeep wheeled it around the front of the truck and disappeared from sight.

Knockknockknock.

David started, again confused to find that life remained on the planet. Slowly, as if all his nerves were disorganized, he went to the door.

Queenie followed, and Chad would have, too, but as he turned, a folded square of paper on the table caught his eye. The paper was pale green and looked handmade. There were yellow flower petals pressed into it, and a short word, in purple ink. Chad took a step closer, and yes, it was his name.

Outside in the yard Jeep was saying, "Found this in the back of the barn this morning. I remember when all I wanted in the world was a goat to pull it."

David's heavy voice lifted in an effort at courtesy, a question, and Jeep said, "I'm seventy years old. Better snap to and do it if I'm going to."

"Chad," the purple ink said. It was for him.

"You ever train a goat?" Jeep asked, outside the window.

"Do you have a goat?" David was starting to sound a little interested.

Jeep lured him along. "Know where I can get one! Oh, 'fore I forget, Mother thought you might feel kind of all-on-your-ownsome. You're to come up to supper tonight. But this goat: Is a doe all right? I can come by a culled milker pretty easy."

"A doe should be fine."

Next Jeep would take David off in his truck, that magic solace for all ills. When Julia'd outgrown her pony, when Chad was pinched by being the middle child, when no one wanted to play with Sky, Jeep had taken each along in the truck, and things had gotten better. He'd go off with David, and David would forget this note until at least tomorrow.

Chad couldn't wait that long. He couldn't. "Chad," it said in purple letters, her handwriting, which he'd never seen before, and so the square of paper belonged to him already, and here in the empty kitchen was the place to open it. It was probably one more iteration of the math problem: No matter how it's calculated, you are one year younger than I am, and so good-bye. He'd turn red at the very least. . . . Best open it alone.

He unfolded the paper square.

For a moment he thought there was nothing. Then he saw the small track across the center of the square, written in green felt-tipped pen barely darker than the paper, as if she weren't quite sure she wanted to do this.

lsb@shazamnet.com

Her e-mail address.